# Fuente

## by Cusi Cram

A SAMUEL FRENCH ACTING EDITION

NEW YORK HOLLYWOOD LONDON TORONTO

SAMUELFRENCH.COM

## IMPORTANT BILLING AND CREDIT REQUIREMENTS

All producers of *FUENTE must* give credit to the Author of the Play in all programs distributed in connection with performances of the Play, and in all instances in which the title of the Play appears for the purposes of advertising, publicizing or otherwise exploiting the Play and/ or a production. The name of the Author *must* appear on a separate line on which no other name appears, immediately following the title and *must* appear in size of type not less than fifty percent of the size of the title type.

*FUENTE* was first produced in 2005 by Barrington Stage Company, (Sheffield, Massachusetts) with Julianne Boyd, Artistic Director. The production was directed by Sturgis Warner, with the following cast and creative team:

ESTÉBAN/GUSTAVO . . . . . . . . . . . . . . . . . . . . . . . . . . . . . . Paolo Andino
SOLEDAD . . . . . . . . . . . . . . . . . . . . . . . . . . . . . . . . . . . . . Lucia Brawley
CHAPARRO/ PADRE GUSTAVO. . . . . . . . . . . . . Michael Ray Escamilla
ADELA. . . . . . . . . . . . . . . . . . . . . . . . . . . . . . . . . . . . . . Zabryna Guevara
OMAR. . . . . . . . . . . . . . . . . . . . . . . . . . . . . . . . . . . . . . . . . Piter Marek
BLAIR-MARIA. . . . . . . . . . . . . . . . . . . . . . . . . . . . . . . Jeanine Serralles

Set Design - Brian Prather
Costume Design - Guy Lee Bailey
Lighting Designer - D. Benjamin Courtney
Dramaturge - Alexis Greene

## CHARACTERS

**CHAPARRO/ PADRE GUSTAVO**
**SOLEDAD**
**ESTÉBAN/ DENVER**
**ADELA**
**OMAR**
**BLAIR-MARIA**

## SETTING

Fuente, a southern, desert place – not as far south as you can go but south nonetheless.

## A NOTE ON THE ACCENTS

For Chaparro, Soledad, and Estéban, English is their first language but the rhythm of their speech is infused with Spanish. Spanish is Adela's first language. Omar was born in an Arabic-speaking country.

## A NOTE ON THE LANGUAGE

Although the language is poetic, it is spoken quickly and should mirror everyday speech.

# PART ONE
## LOVE AND HAIRSPRAY

*(Blue sky. Clay earth. Dry heat, turning wet.)*

CHAPARRO. North of nowhere. South of bumfuck. East of
your ass. Fuente. It gets all murky clear in my thinking.
It's like the back of my hand and the back of Venus
at once. Fuente. I say, I say to folks who ask, 'cause
everybody thinks they got the right to know where you
from. I say back at them, like they wanna hear, I say,
Fuente. And they, with them grid-line, map charts of
understanding up their fat asses, don't know where or
what the fuck Fuente might be. I know.
It is not a bedroom community. It is not a seaside resort.
It's not Pleasantville or suburbia, or urban decay. It's
not your city, village, or hamlet. It's not a crossroads or
some spookety spook ghost town. It's not on map you
can buy at your Exxon, 7-Eleven type establishment.
It's not a locale, if you get my point.
Fuente is Soledad. And she is un-mappable as a planet
not yet discovered. She is the glass of lemonade with
ice cubicles that you crave in high Fahrenheit heat.
She is all things to anyone who wanted or knew wanting deep. She knows without asking and is mine, all
mine. Mine. My mine. I mine her. I'm rich. So rich,
I get silly. Silly in Fuente. Dry old Fuente. West of any
thought you ever had. Soledad! Soledad!

*(SOLEDAD runs toward CHAPARRO. He picks her up
and twirls her around.)*

SOLEDAD. Where's your truck, silly man?

CHAPARRO. Ran out of gas two miles back but I ran. Ran
to see you.

*(SOLEDAD runs away from CHAPARRO.)*

**SOLEDAD.** Maybe you gotta run some more.

> *(CHAPARRO chases SOLEDAD.)*

**CHAPARRO.** You are a pirate and I'm gonna capture you and take your golden booty.

> *(CHAPARRO catches SOLEDAD and brings her to her knees. She giggles.)*

**CHAPARRO.** You are a sly river fish but I'm gonna hook you this time.

> *(CHAPARRO lies on top of SOLEDAD and kisses her some more. She giggles some more.)*

**CHAPARRO.** You are a doughnut and I'm gonna suck the jelly out your middle.

> *(He sucks her neck.)*

All day.

> *(She giggles yet again. She suddenly stops.)*

**SOLEDAD.** I'm bored.

**CHAPARRO.** What?

**SOLEDAD.** Like, get off me you feel heavy, bored. Like you could crush my bones. Why you such a bone crusher, Chappo?

**CHAPARRO.** Bone? What?

**SOLEDAD.** I'm tired of your face always wanting. Like for once, one time, once, give me a face all satisfied and then maybe, maybe I won't feel all itchy.

> *(SOLEDAD scratches herself.)*

**CHAPARRO.** Itchy?

**SOLEDAD.** Like the opposite of content or pleased as punch. Itchy. Looking to be scratched, just not by you.

> *(SOLEDAD scratches some more.)*

**CHAPARRO.** Careful, you'll make yourself bleed something bad. Cuts turn nasty quick in Fuente.

**SOLEDAD.** *(in a slightly strange British accent)* Stop your infernal chattering, you're giving me a migraine.

(**SOLEDAD** *catches herself, she has never talked like this before.*)

**CHAPARRO.** Infernal? Migraine? What…what kinda words is those?

**SOLEDAD.** My words, my words, that's what they is.

**CHAPARRO.** It's like someone put a tape recorder device in you.

**SOLEDAD.** I feel unstuck. And for the record, it was not something I was seeking. I liked my glue just fine. You. You all sweet and fully-poseable and puppy-boy like. I was more than satisfied with the glue of you.

**CHAPPARRO.** These past tenses are freaking me.

**SOLEDAD.** I swear up and down me, I swear, the weather is getting wet.

**CHAPARRO.** We haven't had weather in years. Just sun and dust. That's what we have in Fuente. Dust and sun 'til you die.

**SOLEDAD.** I know things humid, Chaparro. I visited the shore when I was ten and felt the word they call briny, so I know. (*suddenly realizing*) My hair is curling upwards, like that time I went to the beach, just like that. And it means something. It means a change in weather or plans. And I can't change the weather but I can change my plans. And I been thinking up and down my head, I've been thinking, and I want a life that's all mixed and different than this one.

**CHAPARRO.** And what life is that?

**SOLEDAD.** Like that show Dynasty on the television set. I want an Alexis Carrington life with stapled hair and shoulder pad sex. Can you give me that, Chaparro?

**CHAPARRO.** I…I…don't know.

**SOLEDAD.** Some days I wish your name was Blake, so bad I wish it.

**CHAPARRO.** Blake? I ain't never met no one named Blake.

**SOLEDAD.** But don't you want to?

**CHAPARRO.** What's all this Blakey Blake nonsense?

**SOLEDAD.** Forget it.

**CHAPARRO.** Come on, Soledad. Ain't no secrets between us.

**SOLEDAD.** I don't want your mumblings on the subject. Your lack of object.

**CHAPARRO.** What you just said means nonsense. You look all sideways. And your mouth just got small. Did you drink my home made brew? It's not a lady's beer.

**SOLEDAD.** I ain't a lady, Chaparro. And I don't never drink beer. *(as Alexis Carrington).* Champagne cocktail's my particular poison.

*(SOLEDAD stops herself. She is not quite sure where these words, this accent are coming from.)*

**CHAPARRO.** This some game? Something you read 'bout in a lady's magazine? I can play games. I can be Blake. Look at me I'm Blake. What he talk like? Like this? *(in a real Gringo accent)* Well, hello Soledad, fine weather we're having here at the estate.

**SOLEDAD.** This ain't no game, Chaparro.

**CHAPARRO.** *(trying to kiss her)* My sweet skinned girl, with the flowery smile. Be soft like you usually is. I miss you. This feels like what rheumatism could be. I am full of aches for you, Soledad.

**SOLEDAD.** Poor, Chappo from two towns over. Poor boy.

**CHAPPARRO.** Why you acting all like jelly or wind, like something I can't hold?

**SOLEDAD.** It's my hairspray, I think.

**CHAPARRO.** Your hairspray? I'm lost, lost without a map lost.

**SOLEDAD.** I think my hair spray changed the patterns in my brain.

**CHAPARRO.** Your brain gotta a pattern? Didn't know that.

**SOLEDAD.** I got the hairspray from the Arabs 'cause Estéban's closed early yesterday, I was in town, mostly buying cutlets for your supper. And I stopped in at the Arabs and bought two packs of Juicy Fruit chewing gum and my normal extra hold Aqua Net aerosol branded hair spray. And the bottle looked all normal, 'cept there was the English letters and then some that looked like what Arabic is.

**CHAPARRO.** What you doing using A-rab-looking Aqua Net?

**SOLEDAD.** Then I come home and brushed my hair thirty three times for luck and straightness, 'cause I know you like the straight look.

**CHAPARRO.** It's not me that likes your hair combed straight. I don't care which way your hair might go as long as it's close to me smelling of whatever the smell it always has.

**SOLEDAD.** It's the extra hold Aqua Net that you like the smell of. So, I bought it on account of and for you, 'cause that's what women do. And it didn't work.

**CHAPARRO.** What do you mean?

**SOLEDAD.** Nothing, and I use that word on purpose, nothing could keep the curl out of my hair. The hairspray smelled strange. Strange like cinnamon and Arab spice. And then just now, I started feeling all itchy and I don't know why but I just can't stop thinking about Alexis Carrington and her face all tight and full of confidence and that accent she has from Europe and that she lived in some place called "Acapoolco" before she came back to Denver to ruin her ex-husband for keeps.

**CHAPARRO.** Acapool...Acapoolco? What's Aca...aca

**SOLEDAD.** It's like my head is full of all the 101 things that I don't have and can't even get in this place. And I ain't just talking 'bout stuff, 'cause stuff is stuff. Words like "Paris" and "possibility" keep racing around my head, and all that racing is giving me the biggest headache I ever known.

**CHAPARRO.** What you need is some Aspirin. I got aspirin.

(**CHAPARRO** *rifles through his knapsack.*)

**SOLEDAD.** Ain't that type of head-ache.

**CHAPARRO.** What type is it then?

**SOLEDAD.** Kind that starts at your feet. I been stuck in the same pair of Payless shoes for a long, long time and they make my head hurt. I want new shoes, Chaparro.

**CHAPARRO.** Fine. I'll get some gas, get back in the truck and drive to Oriba, or Cateña, or all the way to Fuente Central.

**SOLEDAD.** Let me go with you. Let me go, Chappo.

**CHAPARRO.** Ain't the time yet.

**SOLEDAD.** *(as Alexis Carrington)* I'll be toothless and on a gurney before you can ever give me what I want.

**CHAPARRO.** I told you not to talk that way.

**SOLEDAD.** Ain't got no choice in the matter. When?

**CHAPARRO.** When what?

**SOLEDAD.** When am I gonna see something sides this dirt road?

**CHAPARRO.** Soledad, we'll go to magical places like from where that accent is from.

**SOLEDAD.** Promise?

**CHAPARRO.** Promise.

**SOLEDAD.** I wish I could believe you, so bad I wish it.

**CHAPARRO.** Believe me. You always believe me, Soledad.

**SOLEDAD.** I want to go somewhere, somewhere with a name that I don't know how to say.

**CHAPARRO.** Maybe that hair spray did do something to you, something strange weird.

**SOLEDAD.** What about my shoes? I was serious about the shoes. Dead serious.

**CHAPARRO.** I have enough for two pair. And after I get them, there will be no more itching or speaking of others to scratch the itching.

**SOLEDAD.** What I want is shoes like a nurse or old lady. Shoes for walking. I have sandals with wide open toes and they have gotten me nowhere Chaparro. Nowhere. Nowhere but Fuente.

*(Lights out on* **CHAPARRO** *and* **SOLEDAD.***)*

*(Lights up on* **SOLEDAD** *she sits outside and drinks a large can of beer.)*

**SOLEDAD.** I swear, I seen three cross-eyed kittens today. And that means something. Something. It ain't good. I remember that much.

*(She crushes her beer can and tosses it out in to the desert.)*

**SOLEDAD.** *(cont.)* Take that you motherfucking bad omen kittens. I got plans. Alexis Morrell Carrington Colby Dexter Rowan plans.

(**SOLEDAD** *is not quite sure where all those names just came from.* **ESTÉBAN** *enters and picks up the beer can. He carries a paper bag.)*

**ESTÉBAN.** Littering ain't legal.

**SOLEDAD.** Like I give two turnips.

**ESTÉBAN.** Where s Chaparro?

**SOLEDAD.** Looking for my walking shoes.

**ESTÉBAN.** Out of town?

**SOLEDAD.** Gone two days. Supposed to be two hours.

**ESTÉBAN.** He teach you how to drive, yet?

**SOLEDAD.** Do I look like I got a car? Do I look like I'm in some red convertible with my hair blowing every which way? *(as Alexis Carrington)* Do I look like I'm about to take over Denver Carrington from that no good, two bit, double crossing louse once and for all?

(**SOLEDAD** *stops herself )*

**ESTÉBAN.** What was that?

**SOLEDAD.** Nothing that concerns you.

**ESTÉBAN.** I'd teach you to drive.

**SOLEDAD.** Yeah?

*(A moment.)*

**ESTÉBAN.** Got you something.

**SOLEDAD.** Don't want it. All presents men give have long strings attached right to their cocks and I'm tired of looking at cocks with strings hanging every which way.

**ESTÉBAN.** Never heard you say that word before.

**SOLEDAD.** Got all kinds of new words in me, Estéban.

(**ESTÉBAN** *reaches into his paper bag and pulls out a can of Aqua Net.)*

**ESTÉBAN.** Been a run on the Aqua Net recently.

**SOLEDAD.** What you want, Estéban?

ESTÉBAN. Nothing.

SOLEDAD. Everybody wants something.

ESTÉBAN. You could say thank you, polite like, like most folks do.

SOLEDAD. *(as Alexis Carrington)* I'm the sort of woman who says damn you, not thank you.

ESTÉBAN. Why you talkin in that accent?

SOLEDAD. Aqua Net won't do me a lick of good 'cause I'm going natural and somewhere else.

ESTÉBAN. Chappo taking you some place?

SOLEDAD. None of your business. What's a cross-eyed kitten mean?

ESTÉBAN. Don't remember quite.

SOLEDAD. Why you never come by when Chappo's here?

ESTÉBAN. Don't know.

SOLEDAD. Say it out loud. Say it so the kittens can hear.

ESTÉBAN. *(yelling to the kittens)* 'Cause you been my friend for as long as I can remember.

SOLEDAD. I am like Alexis Carrington and she has no friends, just girl enemies and ex-husbands.

ESTÉBAN. That show ain't been on in years, Soledad.

SOLEDAD. It's all that's been on my television set. On all three channels, all day and all night. It means something.

ESTÉBAN. Means Chaparro should buy you a satellite dish, like what most normal folks have.

SOLEDAD. It means that I am supposed to do something, for once.

ESTÉBAN. Something's boiling wrong in you today.

SOLEDAD. *(as Alexis Carrington)* You can either love me or hate me. I enjoy it either way.

ESTÉBAN. You been drinking? Never seen you drink a beer from the can. Never seen you wasted.

SOLEDAD. So much you'll never see. Poor Estéban.

*(A moment.)*

**ESTÉBAN.** I should be getting home. Adela's making pork.

**SOLEDAD.** Wouldn't want to miss pork.

**ESTÉBAN.** I could sit for a minute, if you want?

**SOLEDAD.** Long as you promise not to spoil the noise in my head.

(**ESTÉBAN** *sits. A moment.*)

**SOLEDAD.** How many miles your truck got on it?

**ESTÉBAN.** Hundred thousand, I suppose.

**SOLEDAD.** That a lot?

**ESTÉBAN.** Not a little.

**SOLEDAD.** You meant what you said?

**ESTÉBAN.** 'Bout what?

**SOLEDAD.** 'Bout teaching me to drive?

**ESTÉBAN.** Sure.

**SOLEDAD.** I wanna learn. By the ocean.

(**ESTÉBAN** *laughs.*)

**ESTÉBAN.** Ever since I can remember you been talkin crazy nonsense 'bout the ocean.

**SOLEDAD.** This time it's all different.

**ESTÉBAN.** Sure it is

**SOLEDAD.** I ain't joking.

**ESTÉBAN.** You mean right now?

**SOLEDAD.** Later is a word I'm sick to death of.

**ESTÉBAN.** What you saying, Soledad?

**SOLEDAD.** Call me Alexis from now on. You know just what I'm saying, Estéban.

**ESTÉBAN.** I gotta wife who's expecting. I got shipments coming into the store. I can't just leave everything like that.

**SOLEDAD.** Everybody got something they have to leave get somewhere. Alexis Carrington left Acapoolco to go back to Denver and let me tell you it looked a helluva a lot nicer than Fuente.

**ESTÉBAN.** You're talking crazy. This is your place.

**SOLEDAD.** Ain't my place. Don't talk like we're the same.

**ESTÉBAN.** Once you thought that way too.

**SOLEDAD.** You in or out?

**ESTÉBAN.** If you had a family and responsibilities, you wouldn't be asking me what I think you're asking me to do.

**SOLEDAD.** Everyone knows what a good man you is Estéban. Upright. Honest. Chrurch going. Blah. Blah. Blah. Maybe it's time for you to be bad.

**ESTÉBAN.** Bad guys do have all the fun.

**SOLEDAD.** It can't have been fun being so good for so long.

**ESTÉBAN.** Been the opposite of fun.

**SOLEDAD.** Is that a yes?

**ESTÉBAN.** It ain't a no.

> (**SOLEDAD** *looks at* **ESTÉBAN**. **ESTÉBAN** *looks at* **SOLEDAD**. *Lights out.*)
>
> (**CHAPARRO** *runs on stage holding two boxes of shoes in his arms.*)

**CHAPARRO.** I done it! I done it! Soledad! You hear me? Nurse shoes! *(He waves the boxes of shoes in the air.)* Nurse shoes ain't easy to come by in these here parts, none in Oriba, they'd heard of them in Cateña and in Fuente Central they'd just run out. Seems like lots of women are looking for walking shoes. All the stores were out of Aqua Net too. Store lady said women had been complaining of a secret humidity.

> *(calling out)* You are violin and I am going to pluck your stings, one by one. Pluck. Pluck. Pluck. You in the bath? Know better than to disturb you when you in the bath.

> (**CHAPARRO** *sits for a moment.*)

I heard 'bout this nursing shoe outlet store in a bar near Lost River and I drove the 200 extra miles for you, Soledad. 'Cause I known you long enough to know your wanting look. Nothing be changing your wanting look. You shoulda seen the place, like racks and racks of the ugliest shoes I ever known. And the colors was like all different shades of vomit, light brown, beige and like snowy white, like when you vomit on an empty stomach. And I got you one in white and one in beige and the nursing shoe lady promised they would be comfortable and let you stand on your feet for longer than long. And I wanted to get you one of them nursing outfits but I run out of cash. Remember? You remember that? I thought we could play nurse like we did natural – like when we was small. Only then I was the doctor and I gave you breast exams because I scared you and told you little girls was prone to breast cancers. Didn't matter. You liked the exams and smiled. And I loved you for smiling.

*(CHAPARRO stands and holds up the boxes of nurse shoes.)*

*(calling out)* You are a peanut and butter and jelly sandwich and I'm going to eat you up in one big gulp. Soledad?

*(A note falls from the ceiling.* CHAPARRO *reads the note. Lights up on* SOLEDAD.*)*

SOLEDAD. I left with Estéban. Mostly because he has a better truck. And he promised he would teach me to drive, drive by the ocean. All the wetness in the air, the damp nights made me think of the beach and when I was ten. I had the itch to see it again and I figured you forgot about the shoes and got lost in your drinking and living like you do sometimes and I ain't got time for that. I feel gravity everywhere, pulling on my ass and tits and I think that's what other people call getting older and it stinks, for certain. Maybe at the ocean gravity don't exist. I gotta find out. *(as Alexis Carrington)* Backwards Kisses. Alexis Carrington.

*(Lights out on* SOLEDAD *and* CHAPARRO.*)*

*(Lights up on* ESTÉBAN *and* SOLEDAD *in a truck.)*

SOLEDAD. I smell the sea. All the fishies. I smell them.

ESTÉBAN. Five hundred, maybe six hundred miles to go. You don't smell no fishies.

SOLEDAD. You're not fully-poseable, are you?

**ESTÉBAN.** I'm hungry and we're running out of cash.

**SOLEDAD.** Chaparro was fully poseable. Like you could place his thoughts, get him to think your mind. You... you...are different cup of tea.

**ESTÉBAN.** I ain't no cup of tea.

**SOLEDAD.** In this kinda mood you are most certain not my cup of tea.

**ESTÉBAN.** We can't stay in no motel with a satellite dish tonight. Too expensive.

**SOLEDAD.** But I like the diversity of channels.

**ESTÉBAN.** What could that possibly mean?

**SOLEDAD.** I like watching the karate movies and cooking shows. It's like mind h'ordurves.

**ESTÉBAN.** If we stay in a motel. At least, I get to kiss you and touch something.

**SOLEDAD.** Stop the truck. I SAID STOP THE TRUCK.

(**ESTÉBAN** *stops the truck.*)

**SOLEDAD.** You say anything like that ever again and I get out. I walk in these god-damn sandals. I walk to the ocean. ALONE.

**ESTÉBAN.** It's just...it's just...it's just...

**SOLEDAD.** You promised, you promised that you would teach me to drive by the ocean. You gonna break your promise like every person I ever had the misfortune to trust?

**ESTÉBAN.** It's just I thought...I thought this trip was gonna be different. I thought you'd be...different.

**SOLEDAD.** I am different. It's you who's the same.

**ESTÉBAN.** Man, I'm some kinda of dumbass.

**SOLEDAD.** Estéban, I can't get all attached to no one right at the beginning of a new life. I might interrupt the natural flow of eventual happenings. You are helping me change my destiny but that is it.

**ESTÉBAN.** Ain't there no place for me in that place you call destiny?

**SOLEDAD.** Yes there is. A place as my sea-side driving instructor.

**ESTÉBAN.** But I was supposed to be bad on this trip.

**SOLEDAD.** Let me ask you a question. You got the life you want?

**ESTÉBAN.** Who gets that?

**SOLEDAD.** TV people is who. And me. And maybe you too if you just relax a little and let destiny take you somewhere for a change.

**ESTÉBAN.** I left my wife, my wife and two kids.

**SOLEDAD.** I don't know what that's got to do with me.

**ESTÉBAN.** It's got everything to do with you and you KNOW IT! You see some life at the end of this road and I just need to know if I'm in it.

**SOLEDAD.** You see a turban on my head? I look like some genie to you that knows the future?

**ESTÉBAN.** No, you look like you always look. Crazy beautiful.

**SOLEDAD.** Can it.

**ESTÉBAN.** You won't give me an inch, Soledad.

**SOLEDAD.** I thought I told you to call me Alexis.

**ESTÉBAN.** I'll call you Alexis if you call me Blake.

**SOLEDAD.** You ain't no Blake and that's a fact.

**ESTÉBAN.** Just you wait. I can be Blake. Bad, bad Blake.

(**ESTÉBAN** *starts the truck. Lights out.*)

(*Lights up on* **CHAPARRO** *and* **ADELA**. *Lying side by side a kitchen table.* **ADELA** *is six months pregnant. A silence.*)

**CHAPARRO.** I'm sorry.

**ADELA.** I understand. I ain't no beauty queen, right this instant.

**CHAPARRO.** Naw, naw, that ain't the case as it stands, at all. Adela, you somethin' else. Adela the desert cat.

**ADELA.** I don't much care for fucking.

**CHAPARRO.** What?

**ADELA.** I like just lying like this, quiet. Don't matter a hoot you couldn't get it up. I'd just have pretended to enjoy myself, make them screamin' noises. It's harder when you're pregnant.

**CHAPARRO.** But everybody in town, everybody always sayin how they hear you and Estéban makin love like some crazy coyotes.

**ADELA.** In a small town, you gotta maintain a reputation. Gives people something to think about. Otherwise, people get so bored they wind up killing each other. Can you get it up with Soledad?

**CHAPARRO.** Only with her. People think all kinds of backwards wrong thoughts 'bout me, Adela. Think I cheat on Soledad, when I leave town. Truth is, I wish I could. She was the first women I ever had and ain't been able to have no others since.

**ADELA.** And what's wrong with that?

**CHAPARRO.** That I ain't got no choice, no possibility. Makes a man weak, a lack of possibility.

**ADELA.** I think I could be one of them lesbians. I do.

**CHAPARRO.** You don't mean that.

**ADELA.** I am most certain 'bout what I just said. My husband gone and left with the woman I known he always loved and I'm pregnant as they come with something that feels like it must be triplets and I got two small babies at home with big appetites, know what I feel? Sleepy.

**CHAPARRO.** Not sure I'll ever sleep again. I'm gonna get in the truck and find her.

**ADELA.** You can't find something that wants to be lost.

**CHAPARRO.** I miss her.

**ADELA.** Everyone's always missing Soledad. Pretty Soledad with the sad, sad eyes. Sometimes...sometimes...I think I might like to kiss her myself. See what all the fuss is about.

**CHAPARRO.** Don't say things like that.

**ADELA.** She ain't quite of this world. Be like kissing God or a ghost, I ain't never done that.

**CHAPARRO.** You a witch Adela?

**ADELA.** Who told you that?

**CHAPARRO.** Folks say things.

**ADELA.** What kind of things?

**CHAPARRO.** That in the store you know what people want before they ask.

**ADELA.** That be some pretty boring magic, if you ask me.

**CHAPARRO.** Padre Gustavo said you gave him hiccups for a year, 'cause he said one of your babies was fat.

**ADELA.** None of my babies is fat and that's a fact.

**CHAPARRO.** How come in your yard you grow oranges the size of basketballs and some of them is blue?

**ADELA.** Maybe I gotta green thumb that sometimes turns blue.

**CHAPARRO.** Nobody in three counties been able to grow citrus on account of the dryness. And I've been places and I ain't never seen no blue oranges. You know stuff.

**ADELA.** I know a little stuff.

**CHAPARRO.** I knew it! Can you see things, Adela?

**ADELA.** When I got a baby in me, I see the truth of folks actions, sometimes, I don't want to, Chaparro. I can't relax and you supposed to relax when you pregnant, that's what the TV ladies always be saying.

**CHAPARRO.** Tell me something you seen. Tell me this instant.

**ADELA.** I could tell you something. Something 'bout Pacheco.

**CHAPARRO.** Which Pacheco?

**ADELA.** Fuente only got fifty folks in it and only one of them is called Pacheco and he's the Pacheco that's Soledad's brother. I seen you drink your paycheck with him every Friday, since you could hold a bottle.

**CHAPARRO.** Sorry, got mixed up. I know another Pacheco in Oriba. Gotta a tattoo of a fish on his back. Think the fish is a flounder.

**ADELA.** Don't know no Pacheco with no flounder on his back. One I'm talking about was married to Belen and the night before she died, he bought her some roses from Fuente central. He stopped in at the store and asked for peanuts and shaving cream. I gave him two rolls of Bounty instead. 'Cause I looked at him and he was covered with blood. I told Pacheco he might need the Bounty later, that's what I told him. He looked at me like I was crazy and then he looked crazy and then those roses he was holding, turned into a pistol. I saw it all 'cause I was pregnant with the baby before this one. Everybody said Belen killed herself but I know Pacheco the one that did it. I told folks, they won't listen, 'cause I ain't from Fuente. Said she shot herself in the head. Belen was not a happy person. But take some kinda brave woman to blow her head off. Not like Belen, she bought Tylenol like candy and that's how she was planning to go. Pacheco, did it for her early and that's that.

**CHAPARRO.** Why didn't you stop him, Adela?

**ADELA.** Couldn't. Belen was on her way out. I saw it clear with good reception. Ain't no stopping destiny, Chaparro and that's a fact.

**CHAPARRO.** Tell me something, Adela. Anything.

**ADELA.** Don't go chasing something that you got no right to catch.

**CHAPARRO.** That's it? What that is, is FUCKING NOTHING!

**ADELA.** I ain't like some fortune teller up in Fuente Central who's gonna steal your cash and tell up a mess of lies. I don't see no crystal ball here.

**CHAPARRO.** I know what knowing eyes look like.

**ADELA.** Can't tell you something I don't see. Ain't a possible possibility.

**CHAPARRO.** I'd hit you, if you wasn't some kinda pregnant witch.

**ADELA.** And that's another reason, I think sometimes 'bout kissing girls. I'm heading home. Ain't no passion to be had in these here parts, just an angry man been left alone.

**CHAPARRO.** South of the equator bitch!

**ADELA.** Don't matter how South or North you might well be from, don't matter at all, 'cause we was not born in this place famous most of all for dust and we been left by two was born with red clay in their veins and cactus thorns 'round their hearts. Soledad was something to be treasured. You known that since you was ten and met her out by the little muddy puddle they call the

River Fuente. But you kept her all wrong, didn't share her with the world like you promised. Thought you could make her stay with your cock, with them sad shoes from the outlet shop. Ain't those kind of things keep a woman, not a woman like Soledad.

**CHAPARRO.** You don't know how to keep a man, so don't you be all Sunday preaching to me about keeping a woman.

**ADELA.** Ever think maybe I didn't want to keep a man, ever think that thought, Chaparro?

(**ADELA** *exits. Lights out.*)

(*Lights up on* **SOLEDAD**. *She stands outside the car and tries to drain a few drops of water from an empty water bottle.*)

**SOLEDAD.** Sippy, Sippy, Sip. Dippy dip. Shit. No moisture here. Just dirt and heat, like my whole life. Made a wrong turn back at that fork. I told him to go straight. Told him, we was driving away from the sea. Told him I been there and know how it smells. He turned into some kinda Blake for certain behind that wheel. I could use a Mountain Dew. Sippy sip. With rum. Or maybe a Champagne Cocktail? Sounds too beautiful to drink. Adela likes her rum. Takes it straight from the bottle. Chug. Chug. Chug. Shit!

(*Spot up on* **ADELA**. *She holds a bottle of rum and sways to music. She starts to fall.* **SOLEDAD** *reaches to help her. They are both teenagers.*)

**SOLEDAD.** Careful. You're wearing high shoes.

**ADELA.** Don't.

**SOLEDAD.** I was trying to help.

**ADELA.** You can't help me.

**SOLEDAD.** You seen Chaparro?

**ADELA.** No. But I seen my husband looking at you.

**SOLEDAD.** We just known each other since before we were born.

**ADELA.** It don't bother me. I could have anyone at this party. (*She swigs.*) And I would enjoy it. You enjoy yourself?

**SOLEDAD.** You're drunk.

**ADELA.** You're funny.

**SOLEDAD.** No I ain't.

**ADELA.** I see you.

**SOLEDAD.** What you probably see is double on account of all the liquor you chugged up. Estéban should take you home, is what he should do.

**ADELA.** I see you.

**SOLEDAD.** Stop saying that.

**ADELA.** You pretend to be like Crystal.

**SOLEDAD.** Crystal?

**ADELA.** From Dynasty. With the blond hair that don't move in the wind and with the sad, faraway eyes. That's what you pretend.

**SOLEDAD.** I pretend no such thing.

**ADELA.** You ain't no Crystal but you got everyone thinking you is. You're very good.

**SOLEDAD.** Well…you're worse than annoying.

**ADELA.** You know who you really are.

**SOLEDAD.** I ain't never seen a woman drink from the bottle in public before.

**ADELA.** It's a family tradition. This town ain't big enough for two Alexisesssss…Know what I mean?

**SOLEDAD.** I'm afraid I don't.

**ADELA.** Don't Crystal me, Alexis.

**SOLEDAD.** I don't know what you're talking about.

**ADELA.** Means, don't mess with me, niña. I look at you sideways, your teeth could fall out. If I sneeze the wrong way, you could lose that silky hair. And you'd be one ugly bald lady. Thing is this: I don't care 'bout you, you and Estéban. Go ahead. You can't hurt me, remember that.

(**ADELA** *begins to exit.* **SOLEDAD** *stops her.*)

**SOLEDAD.** I ain't afraid of you. I ain't afraid of no one. And I'm going somewhere. I'm going someplace all better and different than this one. You hear me?

**ADELA.** I heard you alright, Alexis.

(*Lights out on* **ADELA**. *Lights up on* **SOLEDAD** *by the car.*)

**SOLEDAD.** And look at this more than nowhere I got to.

*(Lights out on* **SOLEDAD.***)*

*(Lights up on* **OMAR.** *He stands behind a counter.* **OMAR** *runs a general store.* **OMAR** *plays checkers with himself.* **CHAPARRO** *enters.)*

**CHAPARRO.** Give me every can of motherfucking Aqua Net you got.

**OMAR.** You usually buy from Estéban.

**CHAPARRO.** Maybe you ain't heard, Omar Caramba, whatever you're idiot-wrong name is, Estéban left town.

**OMAR.** I heard. But Adela's running the store.

**CHAPARRO.** I ain't giving that south of the Equator bitch witch one single cent of mine. Get me a Mountain Dew.

**OMAR.** I don't have any Mountain Dew. Seven Up, Sprite, Fresca, Gingerale.

**CHAPARRO.** Now is Gingerale anything like Mountain Dew to you?

**OMAR.** Wouldn't know. My mother always said soda thins your blood. Don't drink it.

**CHAPARRO.** But you sell it to other people and let them go walking every which way with their blood all thin?

**OMAR.** I figure if their mother's didn't tell them…

**CHAPARRO.** Well it pisses me off to no end that you don't got no Mountain Dew. 'Cause everybody who's from Fuente, knows that if you're from Fuente, you drink Mountain Dew and rum.

*(***CHAPARRO** *takes a swig of rum from a flask.)*

Where's my Aqua Net?

**OMAR.** What you want Aqua Net for? I hear she left, left with Estéban.

**CHAPARRO.** That what you heard? Well, maybe she's coming back. You heard that?

**OMAR.** Nope.

**CHAPARRO.** Well goes to show you that what you know is nothing. *(noticing the checkers)* You always play just you?

**OMAR.** Mostly. Hard to find someone who wants to play. And if you play by yourself you always win.

**CHAPARRO.** Dominoes is my game. Checker's for pussies.

(**OMAR** *places ten cans of Aqua Net on the counter.*)

**OMAR.** That'll be $32.48.

**CHAPARRO.** What did you just say?

**OMAR.** I said that would be $32.48.

**CHAPARRO.** You greedy son of an Oh...Oh...Mar. If you think, if you think for one second I'm going to give you $32.48 for that shit, you are out of your bird brained, A-rab mind.

**OMAR.** Then don't.

**CHAPARRO.** Excuse me?

**OMAR.** I didn't ask you to buy ten cans of Aqua Net.

**CHAPARRO.** Excuse me? I am not comprehending you're chit chat. Give me a Mountain Dew.

**OMAR.** I told you before, Chaparro. I do not carry Mountain Dew.

**CHAPARRO.** Well that just sucks. Know why? I said do you know why?

**OMAR.** Go home Chaparro. Go home and drink some coffee.

**CHAPARRO.** Don't drink coffee, OH-MAR. Do not. Never have. Why does it smell strange in here, Omar?

**OMAR.** Go home, Chaparro. Please. I don't want trouble.

**CHAPARRO.** Smells all weirdy weird. Like curry or some shit. Why?

**OMAR.** I'm closing soon.

**CHAPARRO.** I been thinking, been thinking hard and long and I've come to a conclusion, yes I have. It's all your fault. She said, she said night before she left, she said that the Aqua Net smelled all strange, strange and A-rab. I been thinking you done something, something to the hairspray and you changed her, like in one minute she was sucking my neck and the next minute she was talking about Alexis Carrington and the motherfucking briny brine sea. Why, Omar? What I ever done to your OMAR ass?

**OMAR.** When was the last time you ate something? You look like a hungry dog.

**CHAPARRO.** Just had a banana with Adela.

**OMAR.** Let me fix you a sandwich, Chapparro. I got bologna.

**CHAPARRO.** Sandwich ain't what I want OH-MAR.

(**CHAPARRO** *picks up a can of hairspray and looks at it. He takes the top off and sprays some in the air.*)

**CHAPARRO.** Smells like her. Just like her. Soledad. My Soledad. My one true truth.

(**CHAPARRO** *looks at* **OMAR.** *He sprays the Aqua Net in* **OMAR***'s eyes. Blackout.* **OMAR** *screams.*)

(*Lights up on* **SOLEDAD** *by the car.* **ESTÉBAN** *walks on smiling.*)

**SOLEDAD.** You been gone close to forever and you come back empty handed?

(**ESTÉBAN** *looks at* **SOLEDAD** *and shakes his head and smiles.*)

Where's the friggin' tire?

(**ESTÉBAN** *shrugs and smiles.*)

**ESTÉBAN.** No tire.

**SOLEDAD.** Then why the hell you laughing?

**ESTÉBAN.** Because you peed in my Mountain Dew.

**SOLEDAD.** (*looking toward the sky*) God, when you got a moment please wake me up from this nightmare I'm stuck in.

**ESTÉBAN.** I can't believe you done that.

**SOLEDAD.** What you want from me, I was four.

**ESTÉBAN.** You peed in my Mountain Dew and what I wanna know is why.

**SOLEDAD.** Mamá always said your family was far back related to goats. She was right.

**ESTÉBAN.** You peed in my Mountain Dew and that means EVERYTHING.

(**ESTÉBAN** *sits down and chuckles. This infuriates* **SOLEDAD**.)

**SOLEDAD.** Don't sit. This ain't the time for sitting.

**ESTÉBAN.** I just want to remember how it all went down. I was in the yard playing hoops with Pacheco. And I reached down to take a sip of my Mountain Dew and it tasted funky and WRONG. So, I spit it outta my mouth. And then I looked over and saw your face and you was all dirty and smiley. I knew it was you but you pretended the dog done it.

**SOLEDAD.** What you expect, you was acting like a big-old-full-of-himself seven-year old and that's what you deserved for not looking at me once, not one time. I'd do it all over again right this second, if someone had something that even looked like a Mountain Dew. No tire. No Dew. I hate you.

**ESTÉBAN.** I loved you since that instant.

**SOLEDAD.** You sound all wrong.

**ESTÉBAN.** First time I ever sounded right. I was walking just now and sweating and looking for a gas station, so thirsty and dry I felt like I could split apart and I said why am I doing this? She won't even kiss me. I'm just a ride to her. And then I remembered, I remembered how you peed in my Mountain Dew and how I loved you since that very moment and there ain't a thing in the world I can do about it.

**SOLEDAD.** Nobody but a perv fall for a four year-old who liked to pee where she won't supposed to. You a fool, Estéban.

**ESTÉBAN.** I know. And I'm glad of it.

**SOLEDAD.** Only a certified fool would travel without a spare.

**ESTÉBAN.** Maybe I hoped one day I'd get a flat and the waiting for a ride with you would be the best thing that ever happened to me.

**SOLEDAD.** Mamá was wrong, you ain't descended far back from goats but real close to a donkey.

**ESTÉBAN.** You never told me why?

**SOLEDAD.** Why what, stubborn donkeygoatman?

**ESTÉBAN.** Why Chaparro? You loved me since you was four. But he got you.

**SOLEDAD.** I can't be gotten and that's a fact. And we got bigger problems than that.

**ESTÉBAN.** It's the only problem I ever had. Far back as I can remember, I been watching that man love you, all the while knowing I could do it better.

**SOLEDAD.** Not like you went and became a priest or anything, Estéban. Seems to me, like you did a whole lot of living and loving without me.

**ESTÉBAN.** What was I supposed to do?

**SOLEDAD.** You was supposed to bring back a tire and a Mountain Dew.

*(a moment)*

**ESTÉBAN.** I'm better looking than Chapparro and that's a fact. I wanna hear you say it.

**SOLEDAD.** I always said you was the only person born in Fuente didn't look like a pile of mud. You a handsome man, Estéban. You're the kind of man most women would do a mountain of stupid shit for.

**ESTÉBAN.** Why not you?

**SOLEDAD.** Nothing out there? Not a 7-Eleven, even?

**ESTÉBAN.** Nothing. A whole case of nothing.

**SOLEDAD.** Seems like we found a dryer place than Fuente. I knew you from before knowing and you had so much red clay in you, you was never going to go no place, no place but Fuente. Chaparro came from Lost River. He was like wind or static, moving all the time.

**SOLEDAD.** *(cont.)* Mamma said if I fell for you, the farthest I would ever get would be Fuente Central, if I was lucky. Mamma had a wandering soul. She knew stuff. Ain't no more to the story.

**ESTÉBAN.** Except he took you nowhere.

**SOLEDAD.** Promises look like one thing and then they become the opposite.

**ESTÉBAN.** I took you somewhere.

**SOLEDAD.** You sure did.

**ESTÉBAN.** You ever think about kissing me?

**SOLEDAD.** If I told you yes, would you make me do it?

**ESTÉBAN.** I'd never make you do anything you didn't want to, Soledad.

**SOLEDAD.** Alexis.

**ESTÉBAN.** What's that all about?

**SOLEDAD.** Alexis Carrington would know exactly what to do right now.

**ESTÉBAN.** What would she do about me?

**SOLEDAD.** She'd fire you as her chauffeur, that's for certain.

**ESTÉBAN.** Then what?

**SOLEDAD.** She'd probably slap you. She likes to slap folks.

**ESTÉBAN.** Why you like her so much?

**SOLEDAD.** She gets what she wants.

**ESTÉBAN.** What about you? What you want, Soledad?

**SOLEDAD.** More.

**ESTÉBAN.** More?

**SOLEDAD.** I want more than my tiny share, more places, more people, more food I ain't ever tried before, more words I ain't heard, more languages that sound all strange, more time, more money, more channels on my TV set, more comfortable shoes, and more experiences that I can't even imagine, more life is what I want. More life. *(beat)* We could die here, Estéban.

**ESTÉBAN.** Die together. Is that enough?

**SOLEDAD.** I had just enough my whole life. Enough ain't the same as more.

*(Lights out* **SOLEDAD** *and* **ESTÉBAN**.*)*

*(Lights up on* **OMAR**. *He has a bandage around his eyes. He plays checkers and stops.)*

**OMAR.** What I got now is nothing. Nothing forever. Allah works that way. He takes away everything, leaves nothing behind. I don't care what anyone says, Allah is not a nice man. I wouldn't want to have dinner with him. I wouldn't lend him my car. Adela put tape on the black checkers so I'd know what's what. Not the same. The fun of checkers is the board, the way it looks. All the squares and circles together, checkers always seemed to me to be like the world, lots of shapes moving around, you win, you loose, you're there and then you're not. This nothing is between life and death and I don't care what anyone says. Don't care if I can learn some other "feeling language," 'cause for me the thing that always mattered most was watching.

My mother was a fat woman, four chins fat, but that's how my father liked her. She was fat and smart and my mother, she always said each of us got a sense we love the most, that rules all the others. For my mother, it was taste. She liked sweets, she liked anything dipped in honey or powdered sugar. And my father gave her sweets like diamonds, piles of things that would stick to your teeth. He killed my mother with the four chins with too much sweet.

Me, I like to watch. Best thing about having a store is learning people, learning what brands they veer to. Sugarless gum, or not. Light beer or normal. Heavy or light flow Tampax tampons. I know those things about people and it's like knowing secrets. I got an encyclopedia of secrets in my brain. Nothing to watch now but the past and it looks like a TV with bad reception. Some channels got just shadows. Like Chaparro, I can't recall his face before he sprayed me with the Aqua Net. But I see his shape. He's the shape of one of them baboons on the Learning Channel. My father is a powerful man. He owns four general stores and just bought a 7-Eleven franchise in Fuente Central. He wants Chaparro dead, soon and bad. Mostly, I just want to see my checkerboard again. Mostly, that.

*(Lights out on* **OMAR**.*)*

*(Lights up on* **CHAPARRO** *running in place.)*

**CHAPARRO.** Run. Run. Run and don't look back. Run. Run. Run and cover distance. Run like a coyote. Run like a rabbit. Run like I ran from my Pop when he came at me with that look. Run away, far away from Fuente. Run to where Soledad might be. Run. Run. Run and never come back to this place, this place I ain't from, this place, that brought me nothing but heartache. Run. Run. I ain't from here. Run. Run away, far away. I come from nowhere. My folks were drifters, they lived where they could for no real reason and then died and left me with nothing but all that they weren't. Run. Run. But sometimes you run and run and no matter how hard you try, you end up right at the beginning.

*(Lights up on* **SOLEDAD** *and* **CHAPARRO**. **CHAPARRO** *stares at* **SOLEDAD** *while she erases something from a notebook.* **SOLEDAD** *does not see* **CHAPARRO**. **CHAP-ARRO** *is ten,* **SOLEDAD** *is seven.)*

**SOLEDAD.** *(erasing)* Dear God I didn't mean what I wrote about how I wished my brother Pacheco and my Papá could be eaten by flesh eating worms. I don't want no one I know to be eaten by worms. Please God, I'm sorry I wrote all that. You see me erasing?

**CHAPARRO.** God only listens to rich people. My Papá told me that.

**SOLEDAD.** Well, your Papá looks like he knows just about nothing at all. You shouldn't sneak up on folks. You can give them heart attacks or strokes. Stop staring at me.

**CHAPARRO.** Can't help it.

**SOLEDAD.** Where you from. Really?

**CHAPARRO.** Nowhere.

**SOLEDAD.** Everyone from somewhere. Mamma said you and your own lived in Lost River. I never been there.

**CHAPARRO.** I was born there, maybe. But I only lived there one school year.

**SOLEDAD.** Before that?

**CHAPARRO.** Before that. North. I been on a plane.

**SOLEDAD.** I don't believe you. Mamma said she thought your family looked like gypsies or thieves and if I knew what was good for me, I'd keep my distance. But she also said something weird strange about you.

**CHAPARRO.** What she say?

**SOLEDAD.** Said you was the kind of boy she would fall in love with if she did that sort of thing anymore, that's what she said. You gotta picture of the airplane you rode?

**CHAPARRO.** Yup. Somewhere. I'll find it and give it to you if you let me kiss you.

**SOLEDAD.** I'm too little to kiss and that's a fact.

**CHAPARRO.** How little?

**SOLEDAD.** Smaller than you, I bet. I'm seven and I love Estéban, so I couldn't kiss you anyway. Once, *(she giggles)* once when I was more little than now, I peed in his Mountain Dew and he drunk it up.

**CHAPARRO.** You did not do that. You too pretty to do something so mean.

**SOLEDAD.** I did most certain and I'll do it to you, if you don't behave.

**CHAPARRO.** I could teach you how to kiss, and then Estéban would be all surprised the first time.

**SOLEDAD.** I don't want to kiss Estéban. I want to marry Estéban and that's different.

**CHAPARRO.** Then maybe you can kiss me.

**SOLEDAD.** You got wild eyes.

**CHAPARRO.** Wild for you. I ate snow.

**SOLEDAD.** You full of lies.

**CHAPARRO.** Tastes like ice cream. Up north everyone is all fat because they eat snow all the time.

**SOLEDAD.** You ever seen the ocean?

**CHAPARRO.** No, but I mean to. If you kiss me, Soledad I'll take you to magic places. Places where everyone looks like they from the TV set.

**SOLEDAD.** Papá don't like me talking to boys. Supper is soon and if I talk too much he'll know. My Papá can smell stuff on me. I think he might be related to God, my Papá.

**CHAPARRO.** Why you think that Soledad?

**SOLEDAD.** 'Cause he's everywhere at once. I gotta a secret and I might tell you, if you swear on something that hurts, not to tell one other single person in the entire wide wide world.

*(**CHAPARRO** takes out a pen knife and cuts his finger.)*

**CHAPARRO.** I swear on my own blood, that's the biggest swear there is.

**SOLEDAD.** Wow. Better uninfect that. Dust gets in to it they might have ampertate your finger.

**CHAPARRO.** Tell me the secret, Soledad.

**SOLEDAD.** Mamá is taking us to the ocean. She got maps an money saved and me and my brother Pacheco are going one of these days. She gonna take the truck and leave Papá stranded, and that's a fact not something from my head. I asked if Estéban could come and she said, no. I could ask for you? You want to see the beach, or what?

**CHAPARRO.** Sure.

**SOLEDAD.** I gotta go.

**CHAPARRO.** Lemme kiss you first. Quick and tender like in the movies.

**SOLEDAD.** Just once and never again. Estéban won't like it.

**CHAPARRO.** He'll never know.

*(**CHAPARRO** and **SOLEDAD** kiss, on the lips.)*

**CHAPARRO.** You from heaven, I swear.

**SOLEDAD.** I'm from Fuente and that's a fact. You tell my secret and I'll pee on something you love.

*(**SOLEDAD** exits, running. **CHAPARRO** touches his lips and runs off-stage.)*

*(Lights up on **ADELA** eating a banana. Some banging at her door.)*

**CHAPARRO.** *(offstage)* Let me in Adela. I swear I'll kill you and every one of your little brats if don't let me in this instant.

*(**ADELA** smiles and slowly finishes eating her banana.)*

**CHAPARRO.** I'll bust through this door. I'm starting. Watch me start.

*(**CHAPARRO** begins to throw himself against the door.)*

**ADELA.** I'm coming. I'm coming.

*(She opens the door. **CHAPARRO** holds a sawed off shot gun.)*

**ADELA.** *(pointing to the gun)* Where did you find that sorry looking thing?

**CHAPARRO.** In a gully, outside of town. I picked it up and then seemed like the only place I could go was here.

**ADELA.** Can't think what you're doing here. Police from three counties be looking for your sorry chocolate ass.

**CHAPARRO.** How is he?

**ADELA.** Who?

**CHAPARRO.** You know who. He get better? Tell me I ain't blinded him like from a storybook myth. Tell me that, Adela and I'll go.

**ADELA.** Omar's blind as a bat. Sad like an old man. I always liked him myself, though it wasn't good for business.

**CHAPARRO.** I ain't never in all my years of hard-life living done something so mean. Omar. Shit. He got the face of a baby. What am I gonna do, Adela? Tell me what?

**ADELA.** Only a sorry man comes back to the scene of the crime, only a man can't live with himself on the run.

**CHAPARRO.** Thought I could leave it all behind, all that first love shit and stuff, thought I belonged to nowhere. But this is my place, Adela ain't nothing in the world but this place left for me.

**ADELA.** That's the saddest thought I ever met and I think sad.

**CHAPARRO.** He can't see nothing?

**ADELA.** You burned the seeing part right out of his eye. Aqua Net full of alcohol, alcohol not good for eyes.

**CHAPARRO.** His mood mean?

**ADELA.** Not him. His Dad. Omar's not full of revenge like most folks.

*(CHAPARRO begins to exit.)*

**ADELA.** Where you going, Chaparro?

**CHAPARRO.** I'm gonna do one right thing for once.

**ADELA.** Omar's in the store, right now. Might want to say some kind words in his ear fore you turn yourself in.

**CHAPARRO.** Right. Kind words. Omar. Thank you, Adela.

*(CHAPARRO exits, running. ADELA's baby kicks.)*

**ADELA.** It's alright, sweet thing. Everything's gonna be fine, just fine. I promise. I got a plan. Your Mamá always got a plan.

*(The baby kicks again. **ADELA** looks around her. She looks suddenly frightened and crosses herself.)*

*(Lights up on **OMAR**. His checker board is set up. He stares out. **CHAPARRO** enters. He holds his sawed off gun. The shop bell rings.)*

**OMAR.** Shop's closed. Closed for good. Adela's gonna buy the place from me and turn it to a 7-Eleven. She thinks I might be able to do something around the place, can't think what. Can't sell anything to you, Sir or Miss, whatever you might be, 'cause all this stuff belongs to Adela now and I don't have my sight.

**CHAPARRO.** Omar?

**OMAR.** Oh, God.

**CHAPARRO.** Omar. Shit, Omar. Look at you. Shit.

**OMAR.** Listen, I would get out of here if I was you. My father has people all over the county looking to kill you.

**CHAPARRO.** Oh, man. Omar. Jesus. I didn't know. Didn't think. You understand I wasn't thinking. I'd been drinking since the moment I knew she left. And everything, was like backwards. I lost my logic. You ever lose your logic, Omar?

**OMAR.** Not that I recall. I'm serious, Chaparro. Get out of Fuente, while you can.

**CHAPARRO.** I came back, came back 'cause I need you to understand, understand things. If you understand, maybe one day, you'll find it in your heart to forgive me.

**OMAR.** Enough people been hurt. Just...go. Go and leave me be.

**CHAPARRO.** You ever love a woman, Omar? Like inside out?

**OMAR.** Love was never my thing.

*(**CHAPARRO** touches his gun to **OMAR**'s head.)*

**CHAPARRO.** Someone. Must be someone from the television set that you thought about?

**OMAR.** I ain't afraid to die, Chaparro. If that's what you plan to do. Go ahead, be better than this life. Do it.

**CHAPARRO.** Don't say things like that. Don't. I want you to understand. Someone? Was there ever someone?

**OMAR.** I'm not like most men, Chaparro. I never looked for love. Please kill me. Kill me and I'll forgive you. I ain't brave enough to do it myself.

**CHAPARRO.** Shut up. You – you – keep on confusing me… changing the subject all around. Was there ever a woman you ever thought about and when you thought on her you found a peace in you?

**OMAR.** One woman. One from the television set. She was on the show about the girls in the boarding school. She had a sweet face and looked pretty in her boarding school uniform.

**CHAPARRO.** What was her name?

**OMAR.** I don't recall.

**CHAPARRO.** You don't recall? What kind of love did you have for this girl?

**OMAR.** Wasn't love. I wanted to play checkers with her maybe one day. I mean I thought about that. Her name was Blair. That's her name.

**CHAPARRO.** Blair? Like from the All About Life Show? You wanted to play checkers with her? Man, Omar, you could do better than her.

**OMAR.** Facts of Life.

**CHAPARRO.** What?

**OMAR.** Name of the show was The Facts of Life. Kill me Chaparro.

**CHAPARRO.** I ain't going to kill you, so shut up about it. You ever been with a woman?

**OMAR.** No.

**CHAPARRO.** You lying. You're face just got weird. Who was it?

**OMAR.** Can't tell you.

**CHAPARRO.** I got a gun to your head.

**OMAR.** I'm not afraid to die.

**CHAPARRO.** Well…then…I'll shoot something else, put you in a wheelchair.

**OMAR.** Anything but that.

**CHAPARRO.** Who you been with?

**OMAR.** Adela.

**CHAPARRO.** What?

**OMAR.** She started it all. I mean, I didn't know what we was doing and then we was just doing it. Sometimes, I think all this bad stuff happened to me 'cause I did those things with a married woman. I would have liked to play checkers with Blair more but that just never happened.

**CHAPARRO.** Adela. Wow. For a long time?

**OMAR.** Over a year. She says this baby is mine. I never thought I'd have a baby. Never thought any of this could happen to someone like me.

**CHAPARRO.** You love Adela?

**OMAR.** Adela's good company, I suppose. She's good at checkers and has been real nice to me since the accident, doing all kinds of stuff.

**CHAPARRO.** She's a witch for sure, Omar.

**OMAR.** People say all kinds of things in a small town, mostly I don't listen.

**CHAPARRO.** You do crazy things when you love someone, Omar and that's all there is to explain. Only one thing left to do.

**OMAR.** And what's that?

**CHAPARRO.** You got to shoot me somewhere. An eye for an eye is the only way to set things right.

**OMAR.** I can't do that, Chaparro.

**CHAPARRO.** I'll aim the gun for you and you take something away from me, like I took away from you and then maybe both of us will sleep the night through.

**OMAR.** I'm not a violent man.

**CHAPARRO.** Everybody's a violent man, Omar. You want to make me blind too? Or shoot my feet off. You tell me and I'll point the gun.

**OMAR.** Why are you so mixed up in your head, Chaparro?

**CHAPARRO.** You don't do it, I'll put you in a wheelchair, I swear. And what could be sadder than that?

**OMAR.** Don't say that.

**CHAPARRO.** Nothing sadder than a blind man who can't walk a step.

(**CHAPARRO** *places the gun in* **OMAR**'s *hands and puts* **OMAR**'s *finger on the trigger. Blackout.*)

(*Lights up on* **SOLEDAD** *and* **ESTÉBAN**. **ESTÉBAN** *lies with his hat over his eyes.*)

**SOLEDAD.** Estéban. Estéban. Estéban. You asleep? I think you really is far back related to goats. Only a goat could sleep in this crazy heat. A Handsome goat.

**ESTÉBAN.** I ain't asleep.

**SOLEDAD.** I didn't mean what I said. That's heat talk.

**ESTÉBAN.** Keep talking.

(**SOLEDAD** *goes over to* **ESTÉBAN** *and takes his hat off of his eyes.* **ESTÉBAN** *keeps his eyes closed.*)

**SOLEDAD.** What you doing?

**ESTÉBAN.** Trying to remember your face without looking.

**SOLEDAD.** There's a storm comin for certain.

**ESTÉBAN.** You can see so much with closed eyes.

**SOLEDAD.** Like what?

**ESTÉBAN.** Right now I'm giving you a bath.

**SOLEDAD.** Perv.

**ESTÉBAN.** Oh, you wish you were in this bath. It's a bath made up of ice in one of those big porcelin tubs that go on forever. It got 14 carat taps. And I have a pitcher of cool water I'm pouring all over you. And you're playing with a rubber ducky.

**SOLEDAD.** What's the ducky's name?

**ESTÉBAN.** Luís.

**SOLEDAD.** Good name.

**ESTÉBAN.** And I keep pouring the cool water on to your head, and you squeeze the ducky named Luís. And you then laugh, like deep inside of you. It's a good laugh

(*A moment.*)

**SOLEDAD.** You should get some rocks.

**ESTÉBAN.** For what?

**SOLEDAD.** A fire?

**ESTÉBAN.** Awful hot for a fire.

**SOLEDAD.** *(rapid fire)* It'll get dark and we may need a fire. But it's also gonna rain and that might put out the fire. What you should do is make us a house or tent, so the fire don't blow out. Don't you always need a fire?

*(ESTÉBAN sits up.)*

**ESTÉBAN.** I don't need a thing. Never been thirstier or hotter in my whole life but I'm in heaven.

**SOLEDAD.** My life is a backward joke, I swear.

**ESTÉBAN.** Everyone's life is backward joke. Everyone's life got the same joke ending.

**SOLEDAD.** And what would that be?

**ESTÉBAN.** One thing for certain and that's death.

**SOLEDAD.** Shut your mouth. The wind might hear you and carry your words to God and God might think I wanna die. I don't wanna die God. I wanna start living. I wanna live the way Mamma had it all worked in her head for me. Let me start that living, right this instant, motherfucking God up in your wall-to-wall carpeted heaven.

**ESTÉBAN.** You think cursing at God gonna make him change his plans for us?

**SOLEDAD.** I ain't like you Estéban. I can't sleep and make up stories in this heat that's all wrong.

**ESTÉBAN.** Maybe it's all right. Maybe you just got change the way you're looking at things.

**SOLEDAD.** Death hurts and that's a fact.

**ESTÉBAN.** Who told you that?

**SOLEDAD.** My dead Mamá. In my dreams she tells me to make the best of the miserable time here on earth 'cause what comes next is more miserable and never ends.

**ESTÉBAN.** You listen to her even though she's rotting in the earth? That woman who took all my happiness. Filled your head with trash and longing. 'Course it's miserable where she is, she's in hell for all the hanky pankying she did with your life.

**SOLEDAD.** You know short of nothing at all, Estéban. So, can it with a capital C. Mamá was was better and finer than anyone around her and that's a fact. She took me and Pacheco to the ocean when I was ten. She wanted us to see the horizon all different. To hear what a wave was. She planned that trip for three years, saving from the nothing my mean-assed Papá gave her. She ate hope instead of food to get away from Fuente and the dust that was her life. We was close. So close to a life all better and different than this one. But he found us. Found us like he found everything. Spoiled her dreams, like he always did. He took away hope and gave us cactus thorns and red clay for supper. He stole the sea and I want it back.

**ESTÉBAN.** Why didn't you go after your Mamá and Pops were all dead and gone?

**SOLEDAD.** I thought Chaparro would take me. He promised. I kept hoping, next time he leaves he'll take me with him. But I learned something true, I did. No such thing as hope. There's just running. This was my running. And seems like all I get to do is run in place.

**ESTÉBAN.** Your eyes just got complicated.

**SOLEDAD.** What you mean complicated?

**ESTÉBAN.** Your eyes have a simple look and a complicated look.

**SOLEDAD.** Maybe what you got is heat stroke.

**ESTÉBAN.** Most likely. Last few hours you've been looking at me simple and it makes me dizzy, but good dizzy.

**SOLEDAD.** You're funny, Estéban.

**ESTÉBAN.** Just 'round you. Otherwise, I can't even make my babies laugh.

**SOLEDAD.** I don't want to think about your babies.

**ESTÉBAN.** You're eyes just started to look real, real complicated. Stay simple. Please.

**SOLEDAD.** Maybe I'll start walking.

**ESTÉBAN.** Don't.

**SOLEDAD.** Why not?

**ESTÉBAN.** 'Cause you know like I know, there ain't nowhere else but here. Never been anywhere to go but towards each other.

**SOLEDAD.** Put your hat back on. Your brain is swollen for certain.

**ESTÉBAN.** Simple. So simple.

(**ESTÉBAN** *walks toward* **SOLEDAD.**)

**ESTÉBAN.** Two lips coming together like some kinda strong magnets. Two hearts pressed together, beating like some drums from far away Africa. Two bodies pressed close, the parts touching that matter. Pressed. Let me begin. Please, Soledad.

(**ESTÉBAN** *kisses* **SOLEDAD.** *The sound of thunder and falling rain. The two kiss. More rain. More thunder. A storm.*)

**End of Part One**

# PART TWO
## JESUS AND THE PACIFIC

*(Years have passed. A large cross hangs center stage. Lights up on a chair suspended high in the air. **BLAIR-MARIA** sits in the chair. A huge, white, prom dress is also suspended in the air, just out of **BLAIR-MARIA**'s reach. **BLAIR-MARIA** swats for the dress and misses.)*

**BLAIR-MARIA.** Shit. Fucking shit, shit, shit. Fuck!

*(**BLAIR-MARIA** looks at the cross.)*

**BLAIR-MARIA.** Sorry. *(beat)* I said I was sorry. *(to the cross)* Stop looking at me like that…like…this is nothing…I know…I know…you've been through more. But this is definitely something. Sometimes, I swear, sometimes, I get so sick of your skinny white ass.

*(**BLAIR-MARIA** crosses herself.)*

Sorry.

*(Lights down on **BLAIR-MARIA**.)*

*(Lights up on **ADELA** and **PADRE GUSTAVO**.)*

**ADELA.** Bless me father for I have sinned. It's been forty-eight minutes since my last confession.

**PADRE GUSTAVO.** I know Adela. I know because I heard your confession. And while I appreciate your dedication to the sacraments…

**ADELA.** You gotta let me talk, Padre Gustavo or I might never tell the whole truth again.

**PADRE GUSTAVO.** You seemed fine this morning. And thank you for the muffins. Delicious.

**ADELA.** The trouble is: I got small ears. Where I come from that means you're a liar or a witch. I'm both.

**PADRE GUSTAVO.** Adela, I find that hard to believe. You are pillar of this community – president of the parish council…

**ADELA.** Council should start looking for another President.

**PADRE GUSTAVO.** Nonsense, we'd be lost without you.

**ADELA.** What I mean is: I got no business with God.

**PADRE GUSTAVO.** What...what are you talking about?

**ADELA.** You ever been jealous, Padre?

**PADRE GUSTAVO.** Well...before I took my vows...there was a...special someone and I think I felt pangs...

**ADELA.** I ain't talking about pangs. I'm talking about the kind of jealous that eats your insides up...kind that gives you ulcers, so the only thing that sits in your stomach right is bananas.

I met Estéban when I fifteen, he was so handsome you had to squint when you looked at him.

*(Spot up on* **ESTÉBAN.***)*

It was love at first sight, at least for me it was. But no one told me that loving him would be like loving a shadow.

*(Spot up on* **SOLEDAD.** *She circles the stage.* **ESTÉBAN** *watches her every step.)*

No one told me that his eyes would always be looking past me.

**ESTÉBAN.** Soledad! Where you headed?

*(***SOLEDAD** *looks over her shoulder at* **ESTÉBAN.***)*

**SOLEDAD.** Wouldn't you like to know.

*(***SOLEDAD** *turns away from* **ESTÉBAN** *and begins to walk away.* **ESTÉBAN** *keeps staring at her.)*

You keep staring at me like that, you'll go cross-eyed for certain.

*(***SOLEDAD** *laughs.)*

**ADELA.** And I got sick of it. Seems like Chaparro came to town and took something he wasn't meant to take and ain't nothing been right since then.

*(Lights down on* **SOLEDAD** *and* **ESTÉBAN.***)*

So, I got to thinking that everything would be better if the three of them just went away.

*(ADELA snaps her fingers and* **SOLEDAD** *and* **ESTÉBAN** *disappear.)*

Forever. I got to thinking about how polite Omar had always been to me and he didn't have to be, wasn't good for business. I got to thinking how I wanted my own 7-Eleven Franchise 'cause I heard that's where the money was. I was right about that.

And it all happened like I thought it.

*(a moment)*

**ADELA.** Padre, you gotta promise not to hate me for what I'm about to say.

**PADRE GUSTAVO.** I promise.

**ADELA.** I put a spell on Omar's Aqua Net, one day after we were at it, one day when I knew for sure he made me pregnant. Magic is just making things happen with your mind. It's like real hard, sometimes bad, thinking, Padre. And I got magic in me when I'm pregnant. I can make a storm come out of nowhere. I can make a gun grow by a gully. I can put Dynasty on your television set twenty four hours a day, if I think it'll get me what I want. But my magic couldn't make a man love me who loved someone else.

**PADRE GUSTAVO.** I'm so very glad you confided in me, Adela, this all so colorful, so fascinating, so passionate.

*(ADELA begins to cry.)*

**ADELA.** I didn't want no one to die, didn't want to hurt no one, Padre. I just wanted my life to belong to me again. But magic sometimes takes people for itself.

*(Lights up on* **ESTÉBAN** *and* **SOLEDAD.** *)*

When they found Estéban's body in a gully near El Gallo, the water had filled him up but he was all peaceful and smiling holding a lady's dress his arms. Maybe in the end he got just what he wanted? You think maybe he found his own kind of heaven, Padre?

**PADRE GUSTAVO.** Most likely, Adela, most likely.

**ADELA.** What you think of your parish council president now?

**PADRE GUSTAVO.** I think you have endured great tragedy, Adela. And when tragedies strike, we want to believe that somehow we have control over them, but we must remember we don't. God is the one steering the great wheel of life.

**ADELA.** Not in my car. There are other drivers in my car, Padre. They never found Soledad's body and in certain shadows Blair-Maria looks just like her. I gotta feeling, a strong feeling Soledad is somewhere talking magic thoughts about my girl but I can't hear them. My ears are too small.

*(Lights down on* **GUSTAVO** *and* **ADELA.***)*

*(Lights up on* **BLAIR-MARIA.** *She is still suspended in the chair. She glares at the cross.)*

**BLAIR-MARIA.** I take it back. I'm not sorry. Asswipe. Cocksucker. Motherfucker. *(a beat)* I wasn't saying those things about you, just in front of you. It's not like you ever stop me. *(a moment)* How come you never move your lips? Or cry? Or burp, even? It's always me blabbing away and you...quieter than Fuente on a Sunday night. I got some BONES to pick with you. A whole platter of them. First bone: when you can take a minute from your busy schedule, I'd really like to get down from here. This some kind a joke to you? Some weird-ass prank? I got two words for you: not funny. Another bone: why'd you go and make my Daddy blind? I know he might not believe in you exactly but he believes in some kinda God and never says an unkind word about anyone and that should count for something. Huge bone – this is the biggest one buddy – you got some kind of crazy nerve to give me the frizzies two nights before prom. I am known in three counties for my perfect hair. And nothing, not even special gels from the expensive hairdresser up in Oriba, would make the frizz go away. I even went into Mamá's closet and sprayed some old fashioned hair spray, the kind old ladies wear, the kind that could protect your head from a tornado. I think it's called Aquaknit. It has strange foreign writing on the label. But it don't matter what

it's called, my head still looks like a Brillo pad. Thanks
for that, big time. Another thing, it's not a bone exactly
but a serious complaint: we need a bar in Fuente, OK?.
As it stands now, we gotta drive fifty miles to Catena for
a cocktail. Most kids just buy beer at the 7-Eleven with
their fake ID's but since Mamá owns every 7-Eleven in
two hundred miles, she went and gave pictures to all of
her clerks of me and my friends, I can't even buy one
of them O'Doull fake beers. Drives Tommy nuts. And
I don't even like beer. *(Alexis Carrington voice)* Tequila's
my particular poison, darling. **(BLAIR-MARIA** *is not quite
sure where those words came from.)* I only had it once but it
was it was a good time until…it wasn't. Tommy promised to get three bottles for prom from the package
store in Lost River. Now that's love. That's almost three
hours round trip. That's Tommy. Why am I wasting my
breath on you, anyway? You can't hear me. It's like you
gotta a head cold. A permanent one.

*(Lights down on* **BLAIR-MARIA***.)*

*(Lights up on* **ADELA** *and* **GUSTAVO***.)*

**GUSTAVO.** Adela, there must be a reason, a very specific
reason that you chose to confide in me today? Everything ship shape with you and…Omar?

**ADELA.** Sure. Ain't love all hot and bothered like but I
reckon you only get that once. One thing I know about
Omar is he isn't going to be looking over my shoulder
at some other girl, not even at the TV kind. Thought
that's how I wanted it. But now God is punishing me
for all my crazy wanting.

**GUSTAVO.** How? How is he punishing you, Adela. I need
details!

**ADELA.** This morning, I came home from Mass. It was
real quiet. And I thought, Blair-Maria slept late, she's
got the sleep in her, all the ladies in my family, 'cept
for me on account of my businesses, got the sleep in
them. And I went up to her room and I opened her
door real quiet. And I look in her bed and she's not
there. And then I look up…

**(ADELA** *begins to cry.)*

**GUSTAVO.** And where was she, Adela?

(**ADELA** *weeps and points up.*)

**GUSTAVO.** I'm afraid I don't understand.

**ADELA.** She was sitting in a chair. And the chair was...

(**ADELA** *sobs and points to the ceiling.*)

**GUSTAVO.** Where, where was the chair?

**ADELA.** In the air.

(**PADRE GUSTAVO** *gasps.*)

**GUSTAVO.** The chair was in the air?

**ADELA.** Yes Padre and her prom dress too.

**GUSTAVO.** Oh my. Oh my, my, my. I see. This is HUGE. The levitation of objects is a sign.

**ADELA.** But I don't know what it means. Women in my family cast little spells maybe big spells if they want something bad but no one in my family ever done anything like this before. We don't float, Padre.

**GUSTAVO.** *(under his breath)* I can't believe something like THIS is happening in this one horse, God-forsaken, miserable town where you can't get a good glass of Chardonnay. This is HUGE. It could put me on the map...maybe get me transferred to Rome! *(calmly to* **ADELA***)* There was a priest at seminary who instructed me in these...delicate matters. I can help you, Adela.

**ADELA.** I knew I could count on you, Padre. Omar don't understand. His God is a different God. His God is from India or Arabia, or wherever he's from. Your God is from Fuente.

**GUSTAVO.** Okey dokey, I need to ask you some questions and you must answer them to the best of your knowledge. Does Blair-Maria growl? Hiss? Make animal noises?

**ADELA.** Well, she's grumpy in the morning. She whines a little, maybe stamps her foot.

**GUSTAVO.** And does her body seem weighted by gravity? Heavy? Like a boulder, perhaps?

**ADELA.** No, I mean she can be a little slow, but like how teenagers is. All draggy and what not.

**GUSTAVO.** Like she can't actually move her limbs?

**ADELA.** Like she's too lazy to move 'em.

**GUSTAVO.** Do you ever feel a chill in her room, an icy draft?

**ADELA.** Who ever felt a draft in Fuente? Breezes been on strike her for two hundred years.

**GUSTAVO.** This is serious, Adela. Gravely serious. This is a battle and we must name and then fight…this…this… demon.

**ADELA.** Padre, maybe Soledad is dead and all unhappy and she's playing with my girl's life, same as I played with hers?

**GUSTAVO.** Adela, we don't know what this. But we will, I promise you. I'll be over as soon as I can. I need to find my special kit and the appropriate vestments.

**ADELA.** Give me a little time. Omar's in a mood lately.

**GUSTAVO.** Remember, Adela our God is a forgiving God.

**ADELA.** For someone like me, don't feel like that's a possible possibility, Padre.

*(Lights out on* **ADELA** *and* **GUSTAVO**.*)*

*(Lights up on* **OMAR**, *sitting at a table. He wears dark glasses. He scratches his head. He stops for a second and scratches again. Lights up on* **BLAIR-MARIA**. *She still sits suspended in the chair in mid-air. She looks at the cross.)*

**BLAIR-MARIA.** Why bother.

*(She whistles. She whistles again.* **OMAR** *follows her whistle.)*

**OMAR.** Don't worry, I'm coming. You sound far way. Where are you?

**BLAIR-MARIA.** Up. I'm up.

**OMAR.** Up?

**BLAIR-MARIA.** Like in the air up. Yeah. I'm freaked, totally freaked.

**OMAR.** Don't be freaked. Are you flying?

**BLAIR-MARIA.** Not exactly. I'm suspended. It isn't just me. It's a chair and my prom dress. Every time I try and put it on it flies away from me.

**OMAR.** Tell me about your prom dress.

**BLAIR-MARIA.** Do you get what's happening here?

**OMAR.** What color is it?

**BLAIR-MARIA.** What color is what?

**OMAR.** Your prom dress?

**BLAIR MARIA.** White. I don't know what to do.

**OMAR.** Tell me about your prom dress. What shade of white? There are so many.

**BLAIR MARIA.** It's not snowy white, the kind that has gray in it. *(thinking)* It's the color of butter.

**OMAR.** The sunny colored butter? Or the paler kind?

**BLAIR-MARIA.** Pale butter, the kind with no salt.

**OMAR.** I always liked that color.

**BLAIR-MARIA.** And the sleeves are short and puffy, I think they're called Princess sleeves and it has a scoop neck and goes just to just above my ankle and when I wear it, I feel important.

**OMAR.** I told your mother to get you the best dress in the store because you are the Princess of the Prom. Your grandmother would be so proud. She grew up in a house in Zahre that was so big you had to bicycle from one end to the other. I can't remember if my mother ever showed me a picture, but I see it. Sometimes, I wish you could see what I see.

**BLAIR MARIA.** I think I do, Omu. What are we gonna do about this situation.

**OMAR.** I'm not sure. It's a complicated one.

**BLAIR MARIA.** This week my jumps in cheerleading have gotten higher and higher. Coach said he never had seen anything like it. Now this.

**OMAR.** Why didn't you tell me? You always tell me everything.

**BLAIR-MARIA.** I dunno. I thought maybe I was imagining things. It's just so weird. Should we tell Mamá?

**OMAR.** She'll just get that silly priest over here. If we were back home people would come from five towns away to see you fly.

**BLAIR MARIA.** I'm not flying, it's more like hovering. What does it mean?

**OMAR.** It means you are remarkable. I've always known it.

**BLAIR-MARIA.** Yesterday at cheer leading, I jumped up and didn't come down for a long, long time and finally when I did come down my pom poms stayed in the air.

**OMAR.** Did anyone see?

**BLAIR-MARIA.** Juana Blanca, but she smokes reefer, so everyone thought she was hallucinating.

**OMAR.** Does reefer do that to you?

**BLAIR-MARIA.** Never smoked it.

**OMAR.** I'd like to try it sometime.

**BLAIR-MARIA.** If I tell you where to stand will you catch me?

**OMAR.** Of course.

**BLAIR-MARIA.** Back. To your left. Two steps back. Baby step to your right. Half a baby step to your left.

**OMAR.** On the count of three.

**BLAIR MARIA & OMAR.** One. Two. Three.

*(**BLAIR-MARIA** falls into **OMAR**'s arms. She gives him a kiss on the cheek.)*

**BLAIR-MARIA.** Thanks, Omu.

**OMAR.** When you were small, I would hold you like this. And I would spin you around and around.

*(**OMAR** spins **BLAIR-MARIA** around and around.)*

**OMAR.** And your mother would worry and tell me to stop. *(imitating **ADELA**)* "Blind man can't be spinning a baby."

**BLAIR-MARIA.** You would never drop me.

*(**OMAR** puts **BLAIR-MARIA** down.)*

Is this all because of Mamá?

**OMAR.** What do you mean?

**BLAIR-MARIA.** People in town talk.

*(The sound of a door slamming. **ADELA** enters with a pouch. **BLAIR** jumps to her feet.)*

*(**ADELA** sits down and begins to count money.)*

**ADELA.** Blair-Maria where are you?

**BLAIR-MARIA.** In my room with Omar!

**ADELA.** Omar! Omar! I need to speak to you, right this instant.

(**BLAIR-MARIA** *looks up at the prom dress and it falls into her arms.*)

**BLAIR.** Weird.

(*The chair then falls to ground with a thud.* **OMAR** *flinches.* **ADELA** *looks toward the noise.*)

**OMAR.** What was that?

**BLAIR.** The chair! (*to* **OMAR**) Folks say she was a witch.

**OMAR.** Your mother was many things. Now, mostly she's afraid of God and the poorhouse.

**ADELA.** Omar! I got some trouble in Canteña, need to talk to you about it. Ain't got all day.

**OMAR.** Coming! I was just helping Blair-Maria move something in her room.

(**BLAIR-MARIA** *kisses* **OMAR** *and exits.*)

(*Lights up on* **ADELA** *counting money.* **OMAR** *enters. He watches* **ADELA** *and scratches his head.*)

**ADELA.** Twenty five, thirty, thirty five, forty. Stop scratching. Forty five, fifty, fifty five. Since when you don't understand what stop means?

**OMAR.** (*still itching*) It itches.

**ADELA.** The doctor said the shampoo will help.

**OMAR.** It doesn't.

**ADELA.** Sixty, sixty five. And STOP means STOP! We need to talk.

(**OMAR** *stops scratching and sits down. He takes some checkers out of his pocket and rolls them in his hand.*)

**ADELA.** How am I supposed to think with that noise? The shampoo will help. I'm not sure you use it right.

**OMAR.** I don't like it, smells like tires. What's wrong in Cateña?

**ADELA.** Blair-Maria seem alright to you?

**OMAR.** Perfect. What about Cateña?

**ADELA.** Day Manager's giving me trouble. Pacheco's gonna come and drive you out there.

**OMAR.** You go.

**ADELA.** Better for a man to do it.

**OMAR.** I'm supposed to play checkers with a guy.

**ADELA.** What guy?

**OMAR.** A guy you never met.

**ADELA.** Must be nice your life, playing checkers when you want, taking little naps in the afternoon, don't got a care in the world.

**OMAR.** When's Pacheco coming?

**ADELA.** Soon.

(**ADELA** *rubber bands and stacks piles of money.*)

**ADELA.** I'm telling you, the 7-Eleven in Oriba is a gold mine! I almost got enough for a new franchise. I know the spot, but I'm three thousand short.

**OMAR.** You'll find the money, you always find the money.

**ADELA.** I know but this time, I gotta a crunch.

**OMAR.** Crunch?

**ADELA.** Time crunch. You know that guy used night manage for us in Oriba, the one with the traveling eye?

**OMAR.** How would I remember his eye?

**ADELA.** 'Cause I told you 'bout it a hundred times. Anyway, now he's got dreams, which is good, long as they don't spoil my dreams. See there's this old gas station right at Three Forks.

**OMAR.** I never heard of Three Forks.

**ADELA.** Yes you have. It's the place where they opened the mine back up.

**OMAR.** I have heard of Three Forks.

**ADELA.** Glad you heard of something. Anyway, we could franchise this place in heartbeat but we're not exactly liquid since we redone the Slurpy machines in Oriba. Man in Fuente Central, said no problem. Today he called me and said there was all of a sudden a big-ass problem 'cause the guy used to night manage the store with the traveling eye has cash and is ready to go.

**OMAR.** Let the man with the traveling eye get this one.

**ADELA.** But we're just three thousand short. So...I was thinking.

**OMAR.** *(interrupting)* No. Absolutely not.

**ADELA.** She's got twenty thousand just sitting there in a savings account.

**OMAR.** That's Blair-Maria's money for college.

**ADELA.** What she need college for?. Things look pretty serious with her and Tommy Johnson. I hear a lot of things happen on Prom night, I got a feeling *(turning to the cross and crossing herself)* I don't really have those kind of feelings like I used to and if I feel them, I ignore them.

**OMAR.** Who are you talking to?

**ADELA.** Jesus, I'm talking to Jesus. And you should talk to him sometime too, Omar. He could maybe give you...

**OMAR.** What? What could Jesus give me?

**ADELA.** Grace, that's what. And let me tell you, we could use some in this house.

**OMAR.** I don't know what grace is. And if you touch a single penny of Blair Maria's money –

**ADELA.** What? What you gonna do to me?

**OMAR.** I'll start praying five times a day to Allah, right outside the house in Arabic on my great grandfather's prayer mat. We have enough.

**ADELA.** Don't you know there's never enough in these here parts.

**OMAR.** I'd like a cup of mint tea, please.

**ADELA.** All out.

**OMAR.** But my father sent some up.

(**ADELA** *stacks her money and puts it in a box and locks it.*)

**ADELA.** Don't know nothing 'bout any mint tea. Pacheco be here soon. Maybe you want to change your shirt?

**OMAR.** This shirt is fine for Pacheco.

**ADELA.** You got some spill down the middle. What kind of boss wears a stained shirt? Kinda boss no one respects.

**OMAR.** Well, I'm not really the boss, am I?

**ADELA.** You sound like every man I ever left.

**OMAR.** You never left a man in your life. They all leave you!

*(OMAR begins to leave. ADELA calls out after him.)*

**ADELA.** I'm never making soup for you again!

**OMAR.** Good, because I hate soup.

*(OMAR exits.)*

**ADELA.** 'Cause you can't eat it right! *(beat)* Respectable people eat soup. People that believe in God and go to church and pray for the salvation of their souls eat soup. *(softer)* I bet the Johnsons eat soup three times a day. Johnsons came to Fuente and bought five hundred acres. You buy that much land, you gonna stay. They got plans to build a golf course and some place for old, white people to retire. Imagine that. Right here. Here in Fuente. They're not going anywhere. Nobody's going anywhere. Not like my boys, left home but boys gotta do that or they become the wrong kind of boys. Not my girl. She's stayin' put.

*(ADELA looks at the cross.)*

You hear me?

*(Lights down on ADELA.)*

*(Lights up on BLAIR-MARIA sitting in a chair. Her hands are tied behind her back. PADRE GUSTAVO stands in front of her holding a cross. ADELA holds a rosary and prays to herself. This has been going on for some time.)*

**GUSTAVO.** What is your name?

**BLAIR-MARIA.** You know my name.

**GUSTAVO.** Tell me who you are!

**BLAIR MARIA.** *(to ADELA)* Why are you doing this to me?

**GUSTAVO.** Jesus loves you. Do you love Jesus? Blair-Maria and anyone else who might be here – Answer me.

**BLAIR-MARIA.** Who else is supposed to be here? Is there someone I should know about? Someone in the closet?

**GUSTAVO.** *(to* **ADELA***)* She is very resistant.

**ADELA.** Her father will be home soon. He won't like this.

**BLAIR-MARIA.** Mamá, please make him go away he gives me the creeps.

**GUSTAVO.** You must remain strong, Adela. This is a battle. Pray, Adela. Pray with every ounce of strength you have.

**ADELA.** Dear St. Rita, patroness of lost causes, I pray to you every day 'cause I thought I was a lost cause and you in your great mercy showed me kindness and reminded me that you had a thorn in your head that made the nuns in your convent stay way from you because the thorn smelled real bad but when you died you smelled like roses. Please let Blair-Maria smell like roses. And dear, dear Saint, Agrippina protector against leprosy, storms and demons, help my baby get rid of this floating demon that will ruin her life and stop her from marrying her one true love, Tommy Johnson.

**BLAIR-MARIA.** You think I have a demon?

**GUSTAVO.** I ask you once again, what is your name?

**BLAIR-MARIA.** *(to* **PADRE GUSTAVO***)* I'm Blair-Maria Rita Agrippina Faheed. And you're getting on my nerves. *(to* **ADELA***)* You think I'm possessed? How can you think that? *(to* **GUSTAVO***)* I know things about you.

**ADELA.** Hail Mary, full of grace the Lord is with thee.

**BLAIR-MARIA.** I don't think Mary can help me. But you can, Mamá. I know you know about this.

**GUSTAVO.** Stay focused, Adela.

**BLAIR-MARIA.** *(to* **ADELA***)* Help me understand this magic, Mamá, 'cause I know you got in you too.

**ADELA.** What I know can only hurt you. *(praying)* Blessed is the fruit of thy womb, Jesus.

**GUSTAVO.** Tell us who you are?

**ADELA.** Let him help you, Blair-Maria.

**BLAIR-MARIA.** He should help himself first. *(to* **GUSTAVO***)* I know all about the videos you rent up in Fuente Central.

**GUSTAVO.** This happens. She'll know things about me that no one told her.

**BLAIR-MARIA.** He likes bears.

**ADELA.** Ain't nothing wrong with that.

**GUSTAVO.** Don't listen to her, Adela. Pray. Just pray.

(**ADELA** *prays.*)

**BLAIR-MARIA.** Kind of bears he likes to watch aren't the kind on the nature channel.

**ADELA.** What kind then?

**GUSTAVO.** Our father, who art in heaven. GIVE US THIS DAY OUR DAILY BREAD.

**BLAIR-MARIA.** He likes a kind of man that's called a bear.

**ADELA.** I don't understand.

**GUSTAVO.** Adela! GIVE US THIS DAY OUR DAILY BREAD. I already said that.

**BLAIR-MARIA.** See, there's this kind of real hairy man they call a bear. And Padre –

**GUSTAVO.** And forgive us our trespasses lord as we forgive those who.. who…What comes next?

**BLAIR-MARIA.** Padre Gustavo likes to watch hairy men with big mustaches and long beards do it.

**GUSTAVO.** On occasion I have rented a foreign film, they are artistic, Adela. Artistic.

**ADELA.** What? What's this all about, Padre?

**GUSTAVO.** Beauty. It's about beauty, I love beautiful men… things, Adela. Beautiful flowers, marble, stained glass… God is reflected back to us in beautiful things…in art. The films…the men…the hair it was all artistic.

**BLAIR-MARIA.** Please!.

**GUSTAVO.** Think about our plans. The chapel. The altar. Beautiful things. Trust me, Adela.

**BLAIR-MARIA.** Go ahead and trust him, Mamá. He likes to watch hairy men lick each other all over.

**GUSTAVO.** Forgive me my sins, father and I know that they are grave and serious but in spite of that, dearest father help me to help this poor lost soul.

**ADELA.** I don't want no hair licker near my daughter!

**GUSTAVO.** I ask you once again, what is your name?

**BLAIR MARIA.** *(putting on a demon voice)* My name is Belen.

**GUSTAVO.** What do you want here Belen?

**BLAIR-MARIA.** *(fake demon voice)* I want to rule the world and kill Pacheco my stupid drunk husband, who let me kill myself because he was so stupid and so drunk.

**ADELA.** Stop it, Blair-Maria. Just stop it. She's acting from some demon movie she saw.

**BLAIR-MARIA.** Isn't that what you want?

**ADELA.** I want to you to be happy. I want to you to be happy like no woman in my family for as long back as anyone remembers has ever been. You want to know something? I'll tell you something. You come from a long line of south-of-the-equator witches, the kind of woman no good, normal, God fearing man will marry, 'cause the power you got is too scary. Nothing good can come of it. I ruined my life, your father's life and too many lives to count.

**BLAIR-MARIA.** People in town are always talking bout you and some beautiful woman named Soledad.

**ADELA.** She wasn't that beautiful and none of all that concerns you.

**BLAIR-MARIA.** Maybe it does. Maybe I want to know. What happened to Soledad?

**ADELA.** Believe me, you don't want to know.

**BLAIR-MARIA.** You are the most afraid person I ever met. And you want me to be afraid too.

*(The sound of a car pulling up.)*

**OMAR.** *(offstage)* 'Night Pacheco.

*(**OMAR** enters and scratches his head.)*

**OMAR.** It's too quiet.

**BLAIR-MARIA.** Mamá and Padre Gustavo think I have a demon inside me. They tied me to a chair and Padre Gustavo keeps asking me my name. He asks me one more time, I'll turn into a demon, I swear.

**OMAR.** Untie her.

*(No one moves.)*

**OMAR.** I said untie her!

**(PADRE GUSTAVO** *unties* **BLAIR-MARIA. OMAR** *scratches his head.)*

**ADELA.** Stop scratching.

**OMAR.** Don't. Don't tell me what to do. I want him out.

**GUSTAVO.** Yes, I think we're all little exhausted. This is time for you to be together as a family.

**OMAR.** Don't ever come here again. I know our daughter flies and that her prom dress flies and that she's magical in every way. What I don't know is why the two of you want to stop that and make her have an arranged marriage to a silly football player.

**ADELA.** She's in love with Tommy Johnson.

**OMAR.** You're in love with Tommy Johnson!

**ADELA.** Tommy Johnson's family is putting down roots in this town. Where you from? Some town that got too many letters in its name, a town that no one in Fuente's ever heard of.

**PADRE GUSTAVO.** I'd better be getting back to the rectory. God bless all of you.

**(PADRE GUSTAVO** *begins to leave.* **OMAR** *stops him with his words.)*

**OMAR.** "That you associate anything with God for which no authority has been revealed: then you say of God what you do not know."

**PADRE GUSTAVO.** I'm not familiar with that – what is it a prayer? From your people?

**OMAR.** It's from the Koran.

**PADRE GUSTAVO.** I'll have to look it up. I have a great respect for the Islamic faith. The culture. The mosaics in particular.

**BLAIR-MARIA.** Just go!

**PADRE GUSTAVO.** God bless you, Adela.

**ADELA.** You're the one person I ain't been praying for Padre. Seems like you need prayers more than any of us.

(**PADRE GUSTAVO** *leaves.* **OMAR** *scratches his head again.*)

**ADELA.** You want to know something, Blair-Maria, something "witchy." What your father needs is a salve of boiled chapparal and desert grass. He should wear it all day at the new moon and then maybe he'll give us some peace from all that god damn scratching.

**BLAIR-MARIA.** Can I ask you something?

**ADELA.** I'm tired.

**BLAIR-MARIA.** How come I know just what that letter you're hiding from Omu says?

**OMAR.** What letter?

**BLAIR-MARIA.** One that starts: "Ain't so bad here. One man's prison is another man's Hilton Hotel."

**ADELA.** You been reading my mail?

**BLAIR-MARIA.** Don't have to read it.

**OMAR.** Who is this letter from?

**BLAIR-MARIA.** Man called Chaparro. Saddest letter I ever read without reading.

(**ADELA** *takes the letter out.*)

**ADELA.** This letter ain't left me since I got it.

**BLAIR-MARIA.** Just after Omu said those words from the Koran, I knew the letter like I'd known it all my life.

**ADELA.** *(to* **OMAR***)* See what you've done?

**OMAR.** What I've done?

**BLAIR-MARIA.** Truest part is what he says about Mamá.

**OMAR.** That's enough, Blair-Maria.

**BLAIR-MARIA.** "We was never so different, Adela you and me. Both of us outsiders, wanting in. Both of us prisoners of our hearts. When I finally get outta here, I'll know for certain that I've paid for my sins. Are you paid up, Adela? Are you?

**ADELA.** Ain't that something? You happy now, Omar? She starts doing those monkey tricks in front of other people, we'll all have to move somewhere else and that's a fact.

**BLAIR-MARIA.** So, do you feel paid up, Mamá?

**ADELA.** I feel tired, deep in my bones tired from trying to protect you from things so big that you can never understand.

**BLAIR-MARIA.** Only thing I need to be protected from is you!

(**BLAIR-MARIA** *grabs the letter from* **ADELA** *and runs out offstage. The sound of a strong wind.* **OMAR** *scratches his head.*)

**ADELA.** Wind and itching means a big change. I don't want anything to change big. You hear me God?

**OMAR.** No one can hear you. Wind's too loud.

(*Lights out on* **ADELA** *and* **OMAR**.)

(*Lights up on a desert sky at twilight.* **DENVER** *paces and speaks into a cell phone.*)

**DENVER.** It's smoking. I dunno…smells like smoke. It's an '89 Ford Tempo. Why're you laughing? Fine. Right. Yeah. No, of course I don't have a gun. I'll keep my eyes open then. Sure. See you then.

(**DENVER** *paces. He turns suddenly thinking he's seen something. He lights a cigarette and sits on a rock. After he sits, he thinks better of it and stands. The sound of humming in the distance.*)

**DENVER.** Spooky-ass place.

(**BLAIR-MARIA** *enters with a big bouquet of Chapparal. She hums to herself as she prunes her bouquet.* **DENVER** *stands and smiles.*)

**DENVER.** Hey!

(**BLAIR-MARIA** *looks at him up and down. She sits on a rock. And takes the letter out of her pocket and reads it.*)

**DENVER.** Those are some strange looking flowers.

(**BLAIR-MARIA** *looks up for a second and then continues to read her letter.*)

**DENVER.** Sure is windy. Hot and windy at once. Strange. That.

(**BLAIR-MARIA** *finishes reading and looks up.*)

**BLAIR-MARIA.** Saddest thing I ever read.

**DENVER.** From a friend?

**BLAIR-MARIA.** Don't know him. But now I do from his letter. *(reading)* "After all the years spent locked away from the sky and the sun, I ask myself, over and over would I do it again, kiss that crazy legged seven-year old girl? Would I do it? And the answer is always sure as my heart beating. Yes!"

**DENVER.** Mind if I ask you a question?

**BLAIR-MARIA.** It feels sad in my hand. Feel it.

(*She hands* **DENVER** *the letter.*)

**BLAIR-MARIA.** Doesn't it have a weight, a heaviness to it?

(**DENVER** *holds the letter.*)

**BLAIR-MARIA.** All the folks in my family feel like that. They smile and and eat their dinner, and go to church but they feel heavy.

**DENVER.** It just feels like a letter to me.

**BLAIR-MARIA.** That's because you're an idiot and you know nothing at all.

(**BLAIR-MARIA** *grabs the letter from* **DENVER.**)

**DENVER.** I get what you were saying. I do.

(**BLAIR-MARIA** *picks up her Chapparal and begins to leave.*)

**DENVER.** I'm sorry.

**BLAIR-MARIA.** For what?

**DENVER.** Insulting your metaphor?

**BLAIR-MARIA.** You're not from around here.

**DENVER.** That's for sure. Lot of snakes in these parts?

**BLAIR-MARIA.** Who told you that?

**DENVER.** Man at the triple A.

**BLAIR-MARIA.** That'd be Pacheco and ever since his wife offed herself, he can't be trusted. I'll take a cigarette.

**DENVER.** Sure thing.

*(He hands her a cigarette and lights it.)*

**BLAIR-MARIA.** He may come get your car, he may not.

**DENVER.** Really?

*(**BLAIR-MARIA** gives **DENVER** another long stare.)*

**BLAIR-MARIA.** Funny, you ain't from here, but you could be. You got the face.

**DENVER.** The face?

**BLAIR-MARIA.** Can't explain it, you just have it, or you don't. I have it and it makes no sense, 'cause my parents are both strangers.

**DENVER.** If…if…Pacheco doesn't come. Is there somewhere to walk to?

**BLAIR-MARIA.** Always someplace to walk to.

**DENVER.** Is there a town? A motel? Some place to eat?

**BLAIR-MARIA.** No but there's a 7-Eleven and if you come with me I can get you the staff rate.

**DENVER.** But there's other people there with houses and stuff?

**BLAIR-MARIA.** There are houses. My boyfriend's family is making a development for old white folks. There's gonna be a golf course.

**DENVER.** I hate golf.

**BLAIR-MARIA.** Like I care.

**DENVER.** All this space makes me antsy. *(pointing to the pile of Chaparral)* What's that?

**BLAIR MARIA.** Chaparral. You boil it up with desert grass and then put it on your head at the new moon and your head won't itch anymore.

**DENVER.** Sounds like a whole lot of nonsense.

**BLAIR-MARIA.** Not if you have an itchy head and nothing works.

**DENVER.** Well I don't have an itchy head.

**BLAIR-MARIA.** Good for you. But my Daddy's blind and his head itches and that's a lot for one person to bear. So fuck you!

**DENVER.** Sorry.

**BLAIR-MARIA.** *(looking off toward* **DENVER***'s car)* You sure have an ugly car.

**DENVER.** Well, fuck you back. Where's your car?

**BLAIR-MARIA.** It's coming to me. When I turn eighteen a lot of things are coming to me, like twenty thousand dollars, which is more than someone like you could make in half a lifetime, if you were lucky. And I got a feeling Pacheco isn't coming. I saw him buying a six pack and one of them super-size bags of Ruffles 'fore I came here. Takes a long time for a small man like Pacheco to eat that many chips.

**DENVER.** I'm not sure one thing you've told me is true. You got a look on your face.

**BLAIR-MARIA.** And what kind of look would that be?

**DENVER.** Like you're hiding something.

**BLAIR-MARIA.** Well, you got a look on your face like you're terrified of snakes and you don't now where the fuck you are. 'Tween you and me, it's not a very attractive look.

*(Suddenly, the bouquet of Chapparal starts to levitate.* **DENVER** *watches it rise in amazement.)*

**DENVER.** What...what...the...what....the fuck is happening?

**BLAIR-MARIA.** *(panicky)* Nothing. Nothing is happening. It's the wind.

**DENVER.** But it's...it's hovering. The wind blows things away, doesn't make them hover.

**BLAIR-MARIA.** The wind is different here.

**DENVER.** You are so full of shit.

**BLAIR MARIA.** It happens...stuff like this happens in the desert. You've heard of mirages.

**DENVER.** This is not a mirage! And they happen in the desert in Arabia, not in little shitty towns, that aren't even towns!

*(The bouquet of Chapparal falls to the ground. The two stare at the fallen Chaparral for a moment.)*

**BLAIR-MARIA.** Please, please don't tell.

**DENVER.** Tell who?

**BLAIR-MARIA.** If you go into town and talk, start spilling your scared guts, there could be consequences.

**DENVER.** Consequences?

**BLAIR-MARIA.** I'm the captain of the cheer leading team, Princess of the Prom. I'm almost engaged to the quarterback of the football team. People named Tommy Johnson don't marry girls who fly.

**DENVER.** You fly too?

**BLAIR-MARIA.** And it's quite possible I may never be happy unless I marry him and don't fly. At least that's what my mother thinks.

**DENVER.** You fly?

**BLAIR-MARIA.** What she thinks is usually right. She's one of those people. He'll propose to me at the prom. And I want that. I do.

**DENVER.** You fuckin fly?

**BLAIR-MARIA.** Not really…Today, I hovered. Sometimes, I jump and I stay up there. I dunno.

**DENVER.** You seem young to fly…I mean – to be almost engaged.

**BLAIR-MARIA.** I'm almost eighteen.

**DENVER.** Like I said. Young.

**BLAIR-MARIA.** I'm not positive I want to marry Tommy Johnson. During football season I do.

**DENVER.** Is it football season?

**BLAIR-MARIA.** Just ended. He burns, you know, in the hotter months. He's kind of pink April through September.

**DENVER.** I get it. Lot of pink people where I come from. Pink people who play golf.

**BLAIR-MARIA.** So you won't tell?

**DENVER.** Tommy Johnson that you find him a turn off half the year?

**BLAIR-MARIA.** Nooo – about the Chapparal?

**DENVER.** But it's OK if I have a little man to man with Mr. Johnson?

**BLAIR-MARIA.** Please. This is my life.

**DENVER.** Strange life.

**BLAIR-MARIA.** What's it to you? You're leaving.

**DENVER.** Like you said, maybe, maybe not. Seems like Pacheco is working on some pretty serious indigestion.

**BLAIR-MARIA.** Look, there's something you should know.

**DENVER.** I'm all ears.

**BLAIR-MARIA.** I come from a long, long line of South American witches. So…

**DENVER.** What?

**BLAIR-MARIA.** So…you better watch yourself. I…I…am on the verge…

**DENVER.** Of what?

**BLAIR-MARIA.** Of knowing a lot of crazy shit. Like tonight, I all of a sudden knew what was in this letter before I even read it…So…

**DENVER.** I've always wanted to know the future.

**BLAIR-MARIA.** You…are a very strange man…boy.

**DENVER.** Look, if you have to hide…things…even crazy things from someone you think you might love then maybe you should find someone else, someone who doesn't burn.

*(a pause)*

**DENVER.** Do you really come from a long line of South American witches? That's so cool!

**BLAIR-MARIA.** It'd be cool if my mother would explain any of it to me. The wildest things have been happening to me but I can't control any of it.

**DENVER.** Well…my car broke down right here in the middle of all this nothing, that certainly wasn't in my plans.

**BLAIR-MARIA.** What are your plans?

**DENVER.** I got a scholarship out West.

**BLAIR-MARIA.** What kind of scholarship?

**DENVER.** Marine biology.

**BLAIR MARIA.** Sounds good.

**DENVER.** I'm gonna swim in the Pacific Ocean.

**BLAIR MARIA.** Always wondered what was West of here.

**DENVER.** I can taste my future.

**BLAIR-MARIA.** And what's it taste like?

**DENVER.** Like sea air, fresh apricots and a mountain of possibility.

**BLAIR-MARIA.** You're making me hungry.

*(a moment)*

**DENVER.** Why don't you come with me?

**BLAIR-MARIA.** I can't do that. I'm Princess of the Prom. I'm almost the queen.

**DENVER.** You don't seem like a princess to me.

**BLAIR-MARIA.** Asshole!

**DENVER.** I know what I see.

**BLAIR-MARIA.** Who cares. Your car sucks!

**DENVER.** I never heard of a flying Princess. But I've heard of a queen bee.

**BLAIR-MARIA.** Well – aren't you…*(She is at a loss for words.)*

*(A long, strange, electric pause. **DENVER**'s cell phone rings. He doesn't move to pick it up.)*

**BLAIR-MARIA.** Could be Pacheco.

**DENVER.** He can wait.

**BLAIR MARIA.** Might want to answer it. Gets awful cold in the desert at night.

**DENVER.** Not if you got someone with you.

*(The ringing stops.)*

**DENVER.** Football season is over.

**BLAIR-MARIA.** *(soft)* I don't even now your name.

**DENVER.** Denver.

**BLAIR-MARIA.** That's a place.

**DENVER.** My mother liked some old TV show took place there.

**BLAIR-MARIA.** I'm named after some fat TV actress my Dad thought was pretty and of course the Virgin Mary. I'm not a virgin.

**DENVER.** Me neither.

**BLAIR-MARIA.** *(holding out her hand)* I'm Blair-Maria.

(**DENVER** *takes her hand and holds it. He doesn't let go.*)

**BLAIR MARIA.** What color do you turn in the sun?

**DENVER.** Color of chocolate, the expensive kind.

*(Lights fade on* **BLAIR-MARIA** *and* **DENVER** *holding hands.)*

*(Lights up on* **OMAR**. *He closes his eyes and prays silently. The sound of a whistle.)*

**OMAR.** Thank you, God.

(**BLAIR MARIA** *sticks her head through a window.*)

**BLAIR MARIA.** Coast clear, Omu?

**OMAR.** All clear. I was worried.

**BLAIR-MARIA.** Something's happened.

**OMAR.** I figured. They're looking for you in town.

*(a pause)*

**BLAIR-MARIA.** Omu, I'm not going to be able to go to Prom.

**OMAR.** I understand.

**BLAIR-MARIA.** How do you understand?

**OMAR.** Because all the women in my family have run away from arranged marriages. My mother came from a rich family but she ran away with a poor grocer. Somehow, she ended up in the desert. But she was happy and wise, but fat, so watch out for the sweets. Try to be like her.

**BLAIR-MARIA.** I'll try. I'm going West, Omu. As West as the Pacific Ocean. He has a scholarship. Maybe I'll get one too.

**OMAR.** You must write and describe everything, every color, every sound.

**BLAIR-MARIA.** I'll describe the exact blue of the ocean and how the wind feels on the beach and what a fresh apricot tastes like. I'll describe him if I can find words.

*(**OMAR** takes off his shoe and takes out a folded piece of paper.)*

**OMAR.** You're not eighteen yet but in two months you will be. When I was eighteen my father gave me the same amount and I came here and bought the store. Sometimes, I wish I had gone farther, or all the way back home but I wasn't brave like you. But when you were born, I knew exactly why I stayed in Fuente.

*(**BLAIR-MARIA** hugs **OMAR**.)*

**BLAIR-MARIA.** Thank you, Omu. I'll be right back.

*(**BLAIR-MARIA** exits. **OMAR** sits. A car horn honks. **BLAIR-MARIA** enters in her prom dress, holding a knapsack.)*

**BLAIR-MARIA.** Zip me up, Omu.

*(**BLAIR MARIA** guides Omu's hands to her zipper. He zips her up.)*

**BLAIR-MARIA.** I wanted you to see me in my prom dress.

*(**OMAR** stands back.)*

**OMAR.** You look beautiful! *(beat)* Now go! Go!

**BLAIR-MARIA.** Say goodbye to her...say something –

**OMAR.** I know what to say.

**BLAIR-MARIA.** I'll write the second I get there.

**OMAR.** Before you get there.

**BLAIR-MARIA.** I'll write tomorrow.

*(**BLAIR MARIA** exits. **OMAR** stands for a second. Blackout.)*

*(Lights up on **ADELA**. The cross is off the wall. **ADELA** delicately wraps it a blanket.)*

**OMAR.** What are you doing, Adela?

**ADELA.** Wouldn't you like to know? Why would she wear her prom dress? She's not going to the prom. Pacheco said he had some crappy Ford. If you're going to fuck your life, at least pick someone who has a Japanese car.

**OMAR.** She felt important in that dress.

**ADELA.** *(laughing)* That's a good one. *(beat)* Everybody's always leaving. Estéban, the boys after him, now her. I already left someplace. I can't leave again. But everyone else gets to.

**OMAR.** Not me.

**ADELA.** I'm not really talking to you.

**OMAR.** Are you talking to Jesus?

**ADELA.** No, I'm not talking to him either. He looks too sad. Why aren't there any statues of him laughing?

*(**OMAR** laughs. **ADELA** laughs and begins to cry. **OMAR** kneels beside her.)*

**OMAR.** She had to go.

**ADELA.** You don't have to explain. I left when I was fourteen.

**OMAR.** We were just borrowing her.

**ADELA.** I wanted so much for her.

**OMAR.** I know.

**ADELA.** I done so many things, Omar, so many wrong things, but she was right. I messed up this one right thing.

**OMAR.** You didn't mess up.

**ADELA.** God sees. He sees all the terrible things I've done and he won't let me have nothing, 'cause he knows I deserve nothing. He takes everything away from me that I love. God hates me and I hate me. You should hate me too.

**OMAR.** I don't. And Blair-Maria doesn't either. She just needs to find out what she wants, instead of what you want for her.

**ADELA.** But what I want is better.

**OMAR.** It's an ancient story, Adela.

**ADELA.** I know, I know, I know, I sound like my mother, my grandmother, and every mother everywhere forever and ever.

**OMAR.** I've never thanked you, Adela.

**ADELA.** For what?

**OMAR.** For waking me up. When I met you, I stopped watching and I started living.

*(**ADELA** takes off **OMAR**'s glasses and kisses each of his eyes.)*

**ADELA.** Thank you, for seeing so much and still staying with me.

*(**OMAR** takes off his shoe and takes out a wad of money. He hands it to **ADELA**.)*

**ADELA.** Shit Omar, since when do you have money like that in your god-damn shoe?

**OMAR.** Since I started playing checkers for cash. I'm good, very good. And everyone thinks they can beat a blind man.

**ADELA.** You had that kinda money all the time?

**OMAR.** Yes.

**ADELA.** So you were just gonna let me blow the Three Forks deal?

**OMAR.** I was just waiting for the right moment.

**ADELA.** I don't believe you. Not for one second. Got anything else I should know about in that shoe?

**OMAR.** Not that I want to talk about.

**ADELA.** You something else, Omar. How 'bout a cup of that Mint tea? I'll put it in one of them colored glasses you like.

**OMAR.** I thought there was no Mint tea.

**ADELA.** *(teasing)* It's strange, I just found it.

**OMAR.** And where was it?

**ADELA.** In my bra.

**OMAR.** Anything else I should know about in there?

**ADELA.** Let's go to the kitchen, I'll take my bra off, make you a cup of tea and I'll show you a few things.

(**ADELA** *reaches for* **OMAR**'s *hand. They walk toward the kitchen.*)

(*Lights up on* **SOLEDAD**. *She slams the phone down. She wears comfortable shoes.*)

**SOLEDAD.** Damn! Only thing I asked him was to pick up the phone, evening time, six o'clock. 'Til he gets there. When his scholarship starts, it'll be different. I know that. Know it. Promised myself I wasn't gonna be this way. Swore on a bible, even.

(**SOLEDAD** *puts the phone down.*)

Don't need a phone to talk to him. 'Course I don't.

Hey there my, sweet, angel-eyed Boy, is it better than heaven on that big, open road? How's the new sneakers? I hope four pairs was enough. Don't you worry one little lick that I'll be paying 'em off 'til Christmas. Like I always say to anyone who'll listen, comfortable shoes can change your life and that's a fact.

Had a dream about you last night. Dreamt you finally saw the pile of dust place that made me. In the dream, you looked at the lonely sky and knew, knew deep down it was in your veins, knew that all that nothing was part of your soul too. It looked strange as the moon to you but a moon you remembered from some other life. Fuente.

I know I never did sit down and tell you just where you come from. 'Spose I just wanted to forget that other life – all the heartache I had before you. And I know you wonder sometimes, I seen you wondering. Let me tell you this, my sweet boy: you come from someone who loved me as best and right as he knew certain. You'll be fine, because you got one of them faces, the kind of face that bad stuff don't happen to. Different from me. 'Spose I'm lucky, in my own mixed up way. I floated into this town, floated with you inside my belly smaller than a dime, floated on the back of some wild storm. So you be careful, careful of water out there on that other coast. A crazy storm took your Papá right from my arms, right when I learning what happiness felt like. Water can do that.

It'll be better there, Denver. Better than here. Gulf coast ain't been so bad. Ain't been so great, either. New night manager was looking at me like I was some kind of lollipop. At the end of my shift, I gave him one of your looks, the real vexed kind, now he don't look at me at all. I came running home to show you the look I gave him. The house was so quiet.

What no one ever tells you is ain't the men but the babies they give you that help make you who you really are. Moment I saw you, I knew for certain that all the LIFE I had been searching for since I was a tiny girl, that LIFE was in my own heart...and in your angel eyes. I better go, m'hijo. Better go. You got so much world to see. Backwards kisses.

*(Lights slowly fade on* **SOLEDAD** *as lights come up on* **BLAIR-MARIA** *and* **DENVER***. They hold hands and face a background of Pacific blue.* **BLAIR-MARIA** *slowly floats upward.* **DENVER** *looks up at her, just as their hands are about to part,* **DENVER** *floats up and joins her. Pacific blue fades slowly to black.)*

**End of Play**

Also by
**Cusi Cram...**

# Dusty and the Big Bad World

# Lucy and the Conquest

Please visit our website **samuelfrench.com** for complete
descriptions and licensing information